SIR THOMAS OF CREEKSIDE

G.L. GARRETT

G. L. GARRETT BOOKS

Cover by Marina Saumell

Book Illustrations by G. L. Garrett

ISBN: 979-8-9866980-0-7 (Hardcover)

ISBN: 979-8-9866980-1-4 (Paperback)

Published by G.L. Garrett Books

Visit the author's website at www.glgarrett.com

Dedicated to all the kids who never had a chance at childhood.

CONTENTS

Through a child's eyes, you can travel to worlds you never knew existed.

CHAPTER ONE

A CREATURE COMES CALLING

I N A STRETCH OF woods, as familiar to you as the ones in your yard, or at the local park, a young boy sits in a shaded maple tree with his trusty bear at his side, just as he has always been. He had long been told by his bear that the trees were a good place to hide; to escape the anguish that the adult world tried to burden innocent minds with. It was a place where one could slip away and disappear among the plethora of shiny leaves that huddled together, not only offering anonymity but also providing protection. Protection from the sun and the rain — among other things.

As though being comforted by a million tiny blankets, the pair wrapped themselves within the bountiful green foliage, discussing their world as two friends often do. But for as pleasing as these woods were, not everything is as quaint as it seems. Many dangers lurk within the shadows, fueled by savage tales and ancient lore; ravenous beasts, and demonic goblins; curses and spells. Of course, the reality behind these fables can be altered by the eyes that gaze upon them. A child's innocent stare often casts a different tale than another may.

"We have to go! Every time that obnoxious noise gets closer, we have nothing but problems. You remember what happened during our last encounter with that, that thing," Teddy said, squinting an eye and pointing his fuzzy blue paw at Thomas. "Please! We have to hurry."

"We're not going anywhere!" Thomas sat on the tree branch with his arms crossed. "I'm tired of running. A true knight would never run."

His bear's eyes grew wide. Wider than they had ever been. So wide, in fact, they almost reached his drooping mouth as he tried to wrap his head around these words. "Are you kidding me? You're not a knight, Thomas! Do you realize what'll happen if we're caught?"

"Maybe I'm not a knight yet, but once I defeat The Screech, then I will be. It's my birthright. My father protected the innocent, and so will I."

Thomas stood tall on the branch and gazed off into the distance.

"After I slay the beast, I'm going to change my name to Sir Thomas of Creekside," he said, thrusting his chest out. "Plus, I'm older, so I'm in charge. We stay put."

"Older? We're both seven! And, I'll remind you, mine are in bear years, which are much more than your years."

"That's for dogs," Thomas said as he rolled his eyes and sat back down, adjusting the blue blanket he wore as a cape.

"Uhm, for bears, too. And if you don't believe me, you can look it up when we get somewhere safe. Now, let's go!"

Even though he was just but a tiny blue bear, Teddy had an innate sense of predicting trouble, and his suspicions were more often than not spot on. Because in the distance, the high-pitched, scraping metal noise that started all this appeared once again, piercing through the afternoon air. Unable to control his anxiety, Teddy nervously fidgeted, picking away chunks of bark from the tree as the clanking crept its way closer. Louder and louder, the sound grew unbearable, but Thomas remained still on his branch, unrelenting and disinterested as he swung his legs back and forth. Frustrated by his lack of concern, his devoted blue bear plopped down next to the foolish boy. No matter how scared he was, he would never leave Thomas' side. For as far back as Teddy could remember, he and Thomas shared their adventures. Adventures that were sometimes planned, and other times, such as this, not.

Teddy, as Thomas and his close friends were allowed to call him, or when they were in formal circles, Mr. Ted E. Bear, with an accent on the 'E,' had been a trusted squire for Thomas ever since he was a newborn. Nobody knew for certain what the 'E' stood for, and if you asked Teddy, his answer was always the same: "Extraordinary." Now that he was getting on in years, Teddy was showing signs of his age. His once deep, cottony blue fur had been slowly matted down over the years until it was now barely thick enough to cover his insides. The pretentious bear would tell you he got this way during the great gnome wars of '07, but Thomas knew differently. His companion was just getting older. That being said, Thomas didn't dare contradict him. Any mention of this, other than Teddy's explanation, would cause him to become quite insufferable. But none of that mattered. It was unthinkable for Thomas to give up his little blue buddy and replace him with a new one. They swore an oath to never abandon each other. A stance that was so strong, it had thrust them into the predicament they found themselves in now. But aside from all that, being a bear gave the duo a tremendous advantage for surviving in the woods. With his instinctive skill

3

set, Teddy could gauge what foods to eat, where to hide, what animals were friendly, and, more importantly, which creatures to avoid. The wisdom gained by Teddy was invaluable during their journey into this mysterious, troublesome forest.

"Your stubbornness is going to get us killed."

Teddy had always suspected Thomas inherited his obstinance from his dad, but he was careful not to bring up Thomas' father unless he did. It was too painful.

"Well, I'm of the opinion that the fluff in your head is affecting your thinking. Other than that one tiny, unlikely scenario, when is the last time something bad happened?" Thomas asked as he tried to ease Teddy's fear.

"Tiny?" the bear sputtered as he scrambled to his feet. "We are talking about my nub," he reminded Thomas as he looked back at his rump, giving it a slight wiggle. His round cotton ball tail was barely hanging on by several stitches. "I don't know what kind of bear I would be without my nub. The animals around here have certain expectations of me."

Thomas glanced at Teddy's tail, or what was a bear's version of a tail. The very moment it happened, Thomas knew he would never hear the end of it. The near-tragedy happened during their first encounter with The Screech. Teddy's nub snagged on an old barbed wire fence and was nearly ripped clean from him during their harrowing escape.

"I'm not sure what you're complaining about. It's still there, isn't it? Plus, what could we have possibly done different? We got away, didn't we?"

Teddy rolled his eyes and peeked out toward the woods from behind the trunk of the tree. "That doesn't matter now. What matters is that you're safe, and we keep you that way. And if we don't leave quickly, this may not be the case!"

But Thomas was unmoved. Especially now that the gut-wrenching sound had stopped. As a matter of fact, all sounds that had once filled the forest disappeared; no birds chirping, no leaves rustling, no wind blowing through the branches. However, the problem was no longer the noise. It was the menacing shadow that slowly crept its way through the thick woods, slithering in and out of the elder trees, searching for the next victim to swallow up.

"You should heed his warning, you know? He is quite right," spoke a lazy voice as it struggled to form each word that lingered on his lips.

"Oh, it's you. Figures you would take his side," Thomas said as he spotted Dorian hanging from a tree branch over their heads. Every time they ran into Dorian, it looked as though he had just awoken from a deepened slumber. With his droopy eyes and lethargic smile, you would think Dorian spent most of his days dozing as he nestled in the shade of his pick of maple trees dotting the forest. But Dorian had an uncanny knack for showing up at the most inopportune moments to make sure he expressed his opinions, which were more often than not many, and unsolicited. Not the usual social interaction you would expect from a sloth.

"You see? Even Dorian is saying we need to go. And you know how much he hates to move."

Thomas rolled his eyes. "Fine! If nothing more than to prove you two wrong. Let's go."

Thomas huffed as he leapt off the branch and landed with a solid thud on the ground below. The moment his feet struck the soil, the earth shook, and the trees rustled. Everything in the forest returned to life as the multitude of creatures calling the woods their home scampered to safety.

"Did I do that?" Thomas asked.

"No, of course not. Don't be absurd." Teddy's voice quivered as he looked around. Now feeling the need to whisper, he urged Thomas along. "Let's go this way," he said, pointing to some dense undergrowth.

When they reached the bushes, they dropped to their stomachs and scurried their way under the thick green foliage, lost in the heavy shadows surrounding them. Thomas was quick to reach his hand out from hiding to sweep away Teddy's belly marks dug into the loose soil.

"I told you, you need to suck in your gut when we hide."

Teddy turned his head and scowled at Thomas. "I find that highly offensive!"

Even though they had found cover, it was too late for Dorian to hide, especially at his ridiculous pace. Instead, he hunkered down tight to a nearby tree branch and did his best to blend in, since the eeriness was now upon them. A thundering boom caused everything in the forest to go silent once again. As if nighttime had settled on their little hollow, darkness swept over the landscape. Neither friend mustered up the courage to speak as the slow, creaking metallic noise shattered whatever comfort they were feeling. Thomas squeezed Teddy's hand, as was custom, becoming lost in the soft, warm embrace. As soon as The Screech materialized from the shadows, Thomas felt an explosion of fear erupt through his body, but he would not let this conquer him. A true knight never would. Even as the tears pooled in his eyes and his heart thundered in his chest, he remembered he had his best friend by his side. With his free hand, he grabbed a nearby rock, gripping it tight, ready to do whatever he needed to protect his buddy until the danger passed.

The two friends waited in silence; their faces buried in the ground. Just when Thomas thought it was safe to move, a loud roar broke the stillness as the ground once again rumbled beneath them. They had run from The Screech many times recently, but it hadn't become any easier or any less scary. Thomas and his bear huddled against each other, shaking as they now heard the monster creeping along, mere steps away from them.

CHAPTER TWO

A MOTHER'S LOSS

D ETECTIVE LAURA SPILLEN HAD only been on the police force
for three years. She strayed from the polyester suits of the past,
breathing new life into an old craft. Her predecessor's portraits lined the
halls of the detective's bureau; cigars dangling from their mouths, the gruff,
stoic images that were as outmoded as the building. A far contrast from
the yogurt and granola munching doyen who strode into the office like
a lion marches into a den. For as bright and eager as she was, there were
those certain investigations that turned her into the meek little girl who
bounced from one foster home to the next. A withdrawn child curled up in
the corner of her room, cursing her life, and second-guessing her decisions.
And this was one of those investigations.

As they wound their way through the quiet neighborhood, Spillen
thought back to her first day on the job. The lingering aroma of stale
lunch struggling to cover the musty stench of the bullpen as she walked
into the aged building. It could've been her infectious smile that first
garnered the attention of her peers; an energetic rookie in her dress blues,

outperforming every street cop working the road. But it was her cunning and intelligence that far outshined the young glimmer in her eyes. It wasn't long after her graduation ceremony at the academy, and the badge pinned to her shirt, when the command staff realized how good of an officer she was. By the end of her first year, they had already presented her with several awards and commendations for her bravery and her investigative skills. By her second year, she had been promoted to a detective's position; a first for her department. For as quick as she moved up the ranks, she suffered the murmurs and whispers as speculation swept through the building. But none of that bothered her. She fed on the locker-room discussions like an insatiable beast. Now, to call her anything but detective was a mistake few made.

"That's the address," she said to her partner.

The house was tucked away at the end of a cul-de-sac. Unsurprisingly, it was easy to spot in this formation of cookie-cutter homes. The home strayed from the manicured lawns, white picket fences, and rose gardens that were peppered throughout. It was the black sheep house where the grass was tall and the bushes unruly. Even the assorted flowers in the garden had wilted away, and the crammed mailbox had given up as well, purging its contents on to the ground below. Its worn presence gave the home an undesired uniqueness that was easy to excuse, considering everything that had happened to this woman. As Spillen and her partner trudged up the stairs onto the front porch, her hand weighed heavily as she softly knocked. A young woman in an oversized gray sweatshirt cracked the door open and peeked out. At one time, the detectives would've been welcomed with a broad smile and cheerful greeting. But those days were gone, replaced by red, swollen eyes, and a sorrowful gaze. Any joy once present in the woman's face had vanished, pushed aside and buried beneath an array of worrisome wrinkles. For each time there was a knock on the door, an icy chill shot through her body and froze her heart. A heart shredded from the torturous events that haunted her every moment.

Spillen stood before this woman, dejected. Even if she hadn't known what had happened, Spillen would already assess this woman was not connected to the disappearance of her child. Her disheveled hair and tired eyes gave away her innocence. As heartbreaking as it was, this expression was one that Spillen selfishly wished she would encounter more often. Not because she basked in the torment of someone else's pain, but because it was a begrudging look of purity that reaffirmed Spillen's belief in humanity. Not the one of shame, guilt, or worse, a callous smirk that greeted her each day she interacted with her subjects during their often contentious interviews.

"Mrs. Bristol? I'm Detective Laura Spillen and this is Detective Bushner."

"Hi. Yes, please come in." The woman stepped back and swung the door open wider as the two detectives walked into the house.

"Please, sit down," she said, directing them into the living room.

The woman walked over to the window and slid the thick curtains to the side, letting in some much needed light, which highlighted pictures of a young boy displayed throughout the room. Piles of tissues were strewn about, and a tattered blanket lay warm, wadded up in the corner of the couch.

"Sorry for the mess," the woman told them as she gathered up the discarded tissues.

"Please, don't worry about that. Thank you for meeting with us. Can you tell us how long Thomas has been gone?"

Thomas' mother drew in a deep breath. "The last time I saw him was earlier this morning. He was in his room before I left for work. When the sitter got here, I let her know he was asleep. At least he was when I checked on him. She got concerned when he didn't come out of his room for lunch, so she went in to wake him and — he was gone," she said, closing her eyes as she bit her lower lip.

"Did you two have a fight, or did something happen that would cause him to run away?"

Thomas' mom sighed. "He was acting out in school and here, at home." She sobbed, wiping her tears with a tissue and staring at the ground. "I overreacted. I told him I was going to take his stuffed bear away."

"Is his bear important to him?"

She nodded. "His dad had given it to Thomas before one of his trips; when Thomas was just a baby."

"Is his father available to talk to? Perhaps he's seen Thomas."

She shook her head as a tear slid down her cheek. She dabbed it away before scrunching the tissue in her hand. "No, he was in the military. He died overseas while he was deployed."

Spillen looked over to the fireplace mantle. A triangular folded American flag rested in a display case centered on the shelf.

"I'm so sorry."

She nodded as tears now streamed down her face.

"I knew his bear was important to him. It was just that — I was so frustrated. I didn't know what to do. What made me think that was the thing to say to him?" she said, staring at the detectives. "My poor little boy. I shouldn't have done that. It was so stupid. Teddy is everything to him. Why did I have to do that? This is all my fault."

"It's okay. You didn't mean for this to happen."

Her lip quivered as she furrowed her brow. "It doesn't really matter if I meant it or not, does it? I needed to be stronger. I'm the adult and I need to be there for my child; to be strong for both of us."

The detectives nodded.

"Do you have any idea where Thomas could have gone? A friend's house, or maybe a relative's house who lives close by?"

"No. I checked with everyone we know, as well as the school."

"Do you remember what he was wearing this morning?"

She nodded her head. "I'm guessing he had on a pair of tan cargo pants and a red t-shirt." Thomas' mom smiled, staring at the floor. "That's what I laid out for him last night, and they're not on his dresser now. The shirt had a lion emblem on the front," she said, blindly sketching the image with her finger across her shirt. "In the upper corner. It's like the ones you would see in a castle or on a coat of arms. That sort of thing. We got it for him when we traveled to London."

"Like in a castle, you said?"

"Yes. Thomas became fascinated with medieval knights and castles. That's all he talked about after our trip to the London Tower last summer."

"That sounds amazing. Does he want to go back there?"

She snickered. "Oh, yes. He is always asking us — I mean me — about going back there during his school breaks."

"How old is Thomas?"

"Seven."

"That's such a great age. So, is it fair to assume he wants to dress-up as a knight for Halloween?"

Thomas' mom nodded and smiled. "Of course. It's all he talks about. That reminds me, I didn't see his blue blanket in his room, so I'm guessing he took that too. It's probably tied around his neck, like a cape. He said it makes him feel like he's a true knight."

"Great. Thank you. And you said cargo pants?"

"Tan ones, yes. He wore them all the time because they reminded him of his daddy's."

"Do you think he had his stuffed bear with him when he left?"

"Teddy? Yes, always. He's light blue and has a red bowtie."

"Is there a recent picture of Thomas we can use?"

She nodded and walked over to a bookcase. After pulling one picture down, she started to remove it from the frame, but Detective Bushner stopped her.

"No, please, ma'am. That's not necessary. We don't need the actual photo. I can just take a picture of it, if you don't mind."

"Uhm, yes. Whatever you need." She handed the frame to him and sat down, fixated on the other pictures of Thomas she had displayed on the coffee table.

"What about his room, Mrs. Bristol? Would it be alright if we looked around?"

"Of course, please," she said, standing and leading the detectives to the staircase.

The two detectives followed her up the stairs. She walked over to a door and placed her hand flat on it before she opened it. "This is Thomas' room."

Spillen and Bushner walked into the bedroom while Thomas' mother stood in front of his racecar bed, which was covered with an assortment of stuffed animals.

"He really likes those, doesn't he?"

"He does," she said as she cleared some of the animals away and arranged them on the mattress. "But Teddy has always been his favorite." After she sat down, she grabbed a fluffy gray elephant and squeezed it against her. "His father would always bring one of these back with him from wherever he had traveled. It gave Thomas a special connection to him." She set the animal down and took Thomas' pillow, hugging it tight as she smelled it, trying to hold in her tears.

The room was as organized as you would expect from a seven-year-old. Some of his favorite toys lay scattered on the floor: trucks, building blocks stacked to create a castle, and some picture books. Other than that, everything was in its own place. On the wall was a plastic knight's shield and toy swords. Most of the other wall space had been covered in drawings. On a small desk was a gigantic pile of drawing paper and a massive box of crayons and pencils. Thomas had sketched his stuffed animal friends as they hung out with each other, fighting dragons, climbing mountains, storming a castle with Teddy in a full suit of armor, and several other adventurous outings that came to life in his images. Aside from that, were maps of his own creation, showing different sections of woods and trails.

"He loves to draw," she said, without looking up.

"Hey, Spillen." Bushner called her over to one particular drawing on the wall.

"It looks like a map," Spillen said, taking a picture of the sketch.

The two detectives studied the image. There were several landmarks identified: the Old Cider Mill, Turnaround Swamp, Roland's boat.

"Do you know if this is Creekside Woods?" Detective Spillen asked.

Thomas' mom walked up to them and looked at the drawing. Her forehead crinkled, and she nodded. "When his father — anyway, we would hike along the trails. Thomas also loved to go to the Towers and play on the slides."

"The Towers? Are you talking about Camelot Towers, the big playground in the middle of the woods?"

"Yes. He would jump on his father's back, pretending he was on a horse storming the castle."

"Does Thomas ever talk about going back to Camelot Towers, or the woods?"

She shook her head.

"How about Roland?" Detective Bushner asked. "Does that name sound familiar? Is he a friend of his from school?"

"No. At least not someone that I'm aware of."

"I think I know who Roland is," Spillen said, pointing to one of Thomas' sketches. In the picture, Thomas had drawn a brown frog wearing a top hat and standing alongside Teddy. The caption read, 'Roland and Teddy.' "It looks like he's a frog. Thomas is very talented."

His mom nodded.

The detectives stood in the center of the room and turned, absorbing as much as they could about this world Thomas had created. There were drawings of Thomas and Teddy climbing trees, but most of the pictures were of him and his family hiking through the woods, or swinging on swings, picnicking, just being together. One drawing next to his bed had his father in his military uniform with an American flag behind him and a big red heart above his head.

"Well, you gave us some excellent information, Mrs. Bristol, and we have a picture of Thomas. If it's alright with you, we'd like to put his photo out to the public in case anyone saw him."

"That's fine. Anything that will help find my little boy."

"It will definitely help. We are going to give this to all of our patrol units and post it on our website. In the meantime, if you think of anything else, here's my card. Please, call me anytime, day or night."

Thomas' mom took the card from her and nodded, her face scrunched up as she stared at it.

"Mrs. Bristol, we're going to find him." Detective Spillen said, resting her hand on Thomas' mom's shoulder.

She couldn't speak. All she could do was nod as the detectives showed themselves out.

Once they got back into the car, Spillen turned to Bushner. "How far is Creekside Woods from here?"

"I'd say a good five miles. Why?"

"I can't imagine he could've walked that far without anyone noticing him." She paused and stared out the window. "Regardless, I think we should take a ride through there."

Chapter Three

THE SCREECH

T HE SCREECH HAD NOW drawn close to the frightened duo. So
close, in fact, Thomas and Teddy could smell its revolting breath.
If charred despair had a scent, this would be it. It was a pungent, smoky
breath that didn't give life; it brought death. Secreted within the bushes,
their faces pressed firm against the ground, they remained as silent and
still as a frightened deer. But for as hard as he tried, Thomas couldn't
stop the dirt from scattering beneath him as his body shook. For just on
the other side of their cover, mere inches from their heads, was the beast.

Antagonized and determined, it slowly searched the woods. The sound of its metal sheathing clanking by was almost too much to bear as the beast hunted the duo. It was a horrific brain piercing noise, as odious as nails scratching their way across a chalkboard. All they wanted to do was press their hands against their ears to ease the pain, but they were frozen with fear. The ghastly sound was terrifying. As if by dark magic, the beast's presence swallowed all their bravery and confidence before its grunts finally trailed off as the monster crept further down the path, stalking its prey. A short time later, the clanking became muffled before disappearing into the distance. Thomas unclenched his fist, letting the stone fall from his hand as his body relaxed and they both let out a deep sigh.

"It knows we're here," Teddy whispered as he gave Thomas' hand a comforting squeeze.

"We just have to stay hidden until the Golden Pixie arrives," he reminded Teddy.

"We haven't seen the Golden Pixie for months. What makes you think she will come now? Especially after everything that has happened?"

Thomas shot him a stern look.

"She will come!" he grumbled through gritted teeth as he jumped up and peeked through the bushes. There was no sign of the monster. He turned and leered at the tiny bear. "She promised she would help us if we were ever in trouble, and if I can't defeat that thing alone, then it's the only way we'll be saved."

"You can scowl at me all you want, but like I told you last time, she is not coming. We need to go out there and find her."

Thomas said nothing further as he stomped past Teddy, who scurried to catch up.

"Don't ignore me!"

"You are quite frustrating! I don't know why I bother to keep you around," he said as he secretly peeked out of the corner of his eye to make certain the little bear was able to keep up.

"What sort of creature makes a sound like that?" Teddy asked, fidgeting with his paws and scanning the surroundings. "It's beyond evil."

"The sort of creature I'm in no hurry to encounter again. But if we do, we need to be ready! What about Dorian?"

Teddy looked back, but couldn't spot the sloth. "He always has a way to avoid trouble. And work, for that matter. He'll be fine. Plus, The Screech can't climb."

A voice rained down from the leaves. "I heard that noise it makes is from all the shields."

Thomas and Teddy jumped as Dorian dropped from a branch, landing just behind them.

"Geez, Dorian!" Teddy said, slapping his paw against his chest. "How did you get here so quick?"

"I have my ways."

"What shields?" Thomas asked.

"The shields the beast captured from all the knights who came to slay it. After it defeated them, The Screech gobbled them up in the way, way, way back. Now it wears their armor around its neck like some sort of trophy. It happened so long ago that the metal has rusted, so now makes those horrible noises every time it moves."

Thomas thought for a moment. "Well, I guess that's a good thing. At least we can hear it coming so it can't sneak up on us, but how do we kill that thing if armor protects its skin? Dorian?"

But the sloth was already gone.

"Where'd he go?" Thomas asked, looking around.

Teddy pulled on Thomas' pant leg and pointed up at a tree. On a branch, hidden within the leaves, Dorian was upside down, nestled tight against a limb, fast asleep.

"Impressive," Thomas said, "but not very helpful."

"I told you," Teddy said. "Now, let's keep moving. That thing might come back."

The pair made sure they traveled in the opposite direction of where The Screech had vanished. The journey was long. Creekside Woods was vast, covering hundreds of acres, which provided many places for the duo to hide or escape to. Located at the very edge of town, next to the school and sports fields, it was a popular place for kids to play during recess, and families to hike on weekends. Dense and sprawling, it had an untold number of roads and trails that had been cut through it over the past several centuries. At first, back in the time of the way, way back, as the woodland creatures refer to the past, Native Americans used the land as a hunting ground. They were nomadic. Traveling along the trails, the forest provided them with food and protection. There wasn't much around back then, aside from a few settlements scattered along the river. Later, when more people came to populate the area, the woods became known to the bootleggers, who hid their stills within the dense trees during Prohibition. They cleared their own trails through the forest in order to carry moonshine down to the river for transport. Once Prohibition ended, most of the people left and the woods returned to being inhabited by the animals.

Nowadays, many people use Creekside for recreation. In the fall, the countryside becomes emblazoned with rich red and orange leaves that sweep across the horizon. A favorite destination for hiking from locals and leaf peepers from everywhere else. Later in the year, as the cold arctic air blows in and extinguishes the fall beauty, a new enchantment is ushered in as the snow blanketed landscape plays host to cross-country skiers. But this beauty is in stark contrast to the hellish creature that moves within the shadows, searching, hunting, hoping to steal a child's soul.

"You were in such a hurry to get me out of the tree. Can't you move any faster? We need to make it to Toad Hollow before nightfall."

"My legs aren't as long as yours. And why do we have to go see him? He's not very pleasant."

"Funny. He says the same thing about you."

Thomas stopped and pulled his map out of his pocket. He had created it after the first hike with his parents. Every time they traveled to a new spot after that, Thomas would take out his pencil and sketch the trail along with an image of where they went; an apple and old stone building for the orchard, a deep gorge with jagged rocks for Breakneck Burrows, cattails for Turnaround Swamp, and a boat for Toad Hollow.

"I need to make certain we're headed in the right direction," he said, glancing over at Teddy and raising an eyebrow. "Where did you get all those marks on your nose?"

Teddy stopped and put his paws on his waist. "You know quite well where they came from. We covered this ad nauseam."

Thomas smiled inside. Of course, he knew. Teddy had told him the story a thousand times about how, when he was a baby, he held Teddy close and chewed on his nose. He'd hoped to get the cantankerous bear distracted from their surprise visit to Roland's and focused on something else.

"I don't understand why you like to do this to me," he said, rubbing his nose. "You know I'm self-conscious about that, but apparently you find my disfigurement amusing."

"You're not disfigured," Thomas assured him. "It's our special connection."

"Hmph." That was the only response Thomas received as the surrounding ground became sloshy.

"Great!" Teddy said, trying to shake the mud from his foot. "Why doesn't he ever come to visit us?" he asked, looking down the whole time, hoping to avoid the mud and keep as dry as possible.

"Who?"

"Roland. Kind of pretentious for a frog's name, don't you think?"

"He's a toad," Thomas reminded him. "He's mentioned that a hundred times before."

"Frog, toad, what's the difference? And besides, it's in his name, part of his species, Amazon Horned 'FROG,' but whatever. What do I know?" Teddy rolled his eyes and looked away from Thomas. "Plus, he lives in a swamp," he said under his breath.

"You live in a hollowed-out tree. What makes you so special?" Thomas shot back.

"What makes me so — look at me?" he said, adjusting his red bowtie and holding out his arms. "You don't find this kind of high-quality fur on just anyone. It is very sought after and I do not wish to constantly risk getting it soiled."

Thomas did his best to ignore the agitated bear's complaints.

"Come on. It's just there, over that ridge," Thomas said as he pointed to the hill just ahead.

"We always have to trudge through this mud and slop to get to him. Doesn't it ever dry out around here?" Teddy vexed as he struggled to jump from stone to stone, keeping off of the moist soil. "You'd think he'd return the politeness. I would just like to understand why we always go to him."

"I don't know. What if he has some sort of condition where he can't be away from the water for too long? Anyway, how come you always gripe about this each time we come out this way?"

"Because your failure to read the map correctly allows me time to grumble. You have no one to blame but yourself."

Thomas shook his head as he checked his map once more. The map had seen better days. By now, the construction paper had suffered through rain, mud, streams, tears, and had been stuffed into Thomas' pocket multiple times. So often had it been folded and unfolded that the creases in the paper were separating.

"Hmm. Perhaps we should take some time to draw out a new map. I can make one with more color and sparkle." Thomas beamed as his creativity blossomed.

"Color and sparkle? It's a map, not some sort of masterpiece to be framed. I wouldn't care what it looked like as long as it showed us a way around this slop."

It had become late, and the sky turned a brilliant purplish-blue as the light from the evening stars flittered down from above and speckled across the horizon. The two friends had made it to Toad Hollow by the time the day slowly dissolved into night. Their shoulders slumped and feet dragging along the moist soil, the travelers were physically and emotionally exhausted by the time they noticed the scant light from a rusted oil lamp ahead of them. Even Teddy breathed a sigh of relief knowing they had come upon the swampy home of Roland.

CHAPTER FOUR
TOAD HOLLOW

IN THE WAY BACK, Roland's home had been a bootlegger's steam-powered ferry boat that smuggled illicit bounty along the waterway. But during a spirited run-in with certain fellows carrying badges, the captain of the boat ran aground, and it was abandoned. Over time, the vessel became too run down for anyone to care for, or take an interest in restoring. As far as rundown relics go, it was a fair-sized craft with its large raised wheelhouse and cabin in the center of the worn wooden deck. It must've been quite impressive to see in its day. Now, the aged planks were faded as paint flaked away and holes peppered the hull from rotted boards. The once prominent metal smoke stack had rusted apart some years ago, falling off to the side and lying dormant in the mud. Had it not been for the abundance of cattails and weeds sprouting up all around the craft, it

25

would be easy to spot Roland's house from a distance. But few ventured out this way any longer. After several housing developments were built further upriver, this part of the waterway partially dried up and turned into the muddied swampland it is today. Now the once abandoned boat with its bleached red paddle-wheel became the pride and joy of Roland. He put a lot of work into renovating his home and was quite handy for an Amazon Horned Frog, or any frog for that matter. But even swinging a hammer, he had a certain air to him. His broad mouth, prominent eyes, and subtle horn shaped brow made him rather unique. It was his uniqueness that gave him the wherewithal to consider himself a higher species of "toad." He always touted he was much more than a common frog, and as such, his home needed to be just as unique and opulent. With scrap wood, Roland created an ornate porch. With its gingerbread spindles and turned posts encircling the stern, it gave the dilapidated boat the appearance of an old Victorian home. And that's where the duo found Roland. He looked utterly relaxed, rocking in his chair, wearing a straw planters hat and tan linen vest with a gold watch suspended from a chain peeking out of his pocket. Kicked back with his eyes half-closed, Roland hadn't a care in the world.

"Well, well, look who we have here," he said, watching in amusement as Teddy bounced from rock to rock, attempting to make it over to the porch unscathed.

"Hey, Roland," Thomas announced. "How are you on this fine evening?"

"Apparently better than that bear of yours," he mused as Teddy stepped up onto the porch.

Dismissing Roland's wit, he spent his time trying to scrape the remaining mud from the bottom of his paws.

Roland smirked and shook his head. "It's always a pleasure to have you visit me, Thomas. Please, join me."

Thomas took a seat in the chair next to Roland and began rocking himself in sync with the frog. With the moon and stars providing a soft, warm light, Thomas sat back, relaxed and content. It was a peaceful setting. With the crickets chirping in the background and the slow, steady squeak of the rocking chairs, it was impossible not to be lulled into a state of euphoria. Tiny pops of light flickered across the swamp as the fireflies greeted the evening breeze. The only interruption to the tranquil serenity was the stray fish breaking the water's surface before splashing back down into the still water.

Satisfied his paws were now clean enough to join the others, Teddy made his way over to several discarded crates of moonshine and climbed up on to them.

"Roland." He nodded, refusing to make eye contact.

"Mr. Bear." Roland responded with a cheeky smile. "May I say your fur is looking astonishing?"

He loved to shower Teddy with false praise. It was always near impossible for him to quell his laughter as he watched Teddy's brow furrow.

Ignoring the slight from the outside, Teddy sat on the wooden crates, his legs kicking back and forth as he fumed inside. "Why are we here again?" he asked Thomas.

"Right. Well, there's no easy way to bring this up, Roland, but The Screech is back. I'm worried if we don't find the Golden Pixie, then it will be too late for us. It almost caught us a few times already. Teddy's tail was nearly ripped away from him."

Roland put his face into his hand. "That is awful. But I'm afraid to say she hasn't been back this way. Nobody has seen her for some time. Most fear the worst."

"Do you know where she was last?" Thomas asked. "We can head that way to look for her."

"Hmm. From what I was told, she was last seen around the old cider mill. But that has been several moons ago."

"Do you think The Screech got to her?"

Roland stopped rocking and rubbed his chin, looking up at the night sky. "Hard to say. She's extremely powerful and resourceful, so I'd be quite surprised."

Thomas thought for a moment. "Well, that settles it. We'll go to the cider mill."

"That's quite a distance away, my friend. And it's too dark to travel. I won't hear of it. With The Screech so close, it's not safe for either of you. That monster can see in the dark, you cannot," Roland said. "Stay here tonight. You can continue your search for the Golden Pixie tomorrow. Plus, I have food prepared."

Teddy leapt from the crates. "Stay here? Are you kidding me? This place is being held together by nothing more than termites holding hands."

"You are quite the pretentious bear," Roland said. "You won't find better accommodations for miles."

Thomas interjected before Teddy could cast any further insults. "We would be honored, Roland. Thank you for the invite. I believe my bear is just a little tired and hungry. I'm sure he didn't mean anything by it. Did you?" he asked, shooting Teddy a dirty look.

Teddy opened his mouth, but then his shoulders dropped. "No, of course not," he said, kicking at the wood deck. "What are we having?"

"Oh, my, I've got a special treat for you this evening!" Roland said, jumping off the chair and ushering his guests inside.

Opening the door of the wheelhouse, the aged wood creaked against its rusted hinges. For all his obstinance, Teddy was correct. Aside from the bright, white painted porch, the exterior of the boat had fallen into a state of disrepair. But stepping inside, it was clear to see where Roland spent most of his time, and craftsmanship. The wooden ship's wheel was the first thing that caught your attention. It was polished to a mirrored finish, and the rest of the cabin was just as refined. Lacquered brass oil lamps hung from the papered walls; their light washing the room in a relaxing glow. Hanging prominently in the middle of the cabin was a large brass chandelier suspended from the ceiling by a lengthy chain. Oriental rugs covered the finished wood plank floor. To the side of the room was a cherry wood banquet table. Large enough to fit a dozen guests. The chairs around the table were gilded in gold, and had red velvet tufted padding for the back and seat. Symmetrically hung along the walls were grandiose oil paintings of Roland's family, each member dressed in their finery. But outshining them all was a larger painting of Roland himself. The brilliant gold frame was clearly grander and more pronounced than the rest of the frames in the room. In the image, Roland was dressed in a dark, notch lapel suit. Underneath, he sported his signature tweed vest with a white starched collar shirt and black silk tie, knotted in a perfect Windsor knot. He was leaning against a walking stick with his leg kicked back as he looked off to the side, almost as though he was deep in thought. Teddy started choking as he tried to hold in his laughter.

"My word, is that new Roland?" Thomas asked.

"Oh, my painting? Why yes it is. Nice of you to notice."

Teddy started to say something until Thomas reached over and squeezed his mouth shut.

"It is very exquisite. You've done a wonderful job with the place."

"Why thank you! What is life if you can't live with the niceties the world offers? Now, if you'll excuse me, I'll go retrieve our dinner."

Roland disappeared behind a swinging galley door. Once he was gone, Thomas released his grip on Teddy's face, which released a burst of laughter from the bear.

"Can you believe that pompous —"

"Don't you even think about using those words!" Thomas warned. "Would it kill you to be pleasant for one night?"

"I'm sorry, but look at this place."

As the agitated bear spun in a circle, he couldn't look anywhere in the room without seeing a picture of Roland. Most of them were glamour shots of him in business suits or formalwear. There was even one of him in a military uniform adorned with lavish medals. Teddy stepped over to a mahogany shelving unit filled with books. He took one down and looked at the spine.

"I'll bet you he never once read a book on this bookshelf. And don't get me going on that globe! Where is a frog going to travel? Especially this one," he said, pointing his thumb at the kitchen.

"Toad! For the last time, toad! This place is incredible, and we are very lucky to be invited. So behave!"

The door swung open and Roland walked in pushing a wheeled food cart, piled high with covered silver serving trays.

"Oh, Roland. You shouldn't have gone to any trouble."

"It was no trouble at all, my friend. Please, sit."

Roland set the platters along the tabletop and tapped his fingers excitedly together.

"Where to start?" he asked, standing on his tiptoes before reaching for the first platter. "Ahh, yes," he said, removing the lid. "So, here we have an old family recipe; blackened catfish with spicy rice. Over here, my own special recipe, honey glazed cricket gumbo. In this one there is some cornbread. And last, but not least, garlic roasted okra."

Teddy leaned over to Thomas, holding his paw up and whispering in his ear. "Did he actually say cricket gumbo?"

All Thomas could do was nod with wide eyes as he tried to think of a polite way to decline that particular dish.

"It all looks amazing," Thomas said, carefully choosing his words.

"What's with the large table?" Teddy asked, tucking a linen napkin under his bowtie. "Do you get many dinner guests?"

"You never know who will drop by. So I always like to be prepared. Now, let's have your plates. I'm anxious to hear what you think of my cooking."

Roland dished out heaping servings of each item to Thomas and Teddy before serving himself. He settled down onto his chair and dropped his chin onto his hands, smiling as he stared at his guests.

"Uhm, aren't you going to eat?" Thomas asked.

"Yes, yes, but I am eager to see the enjoyment on your faces when you take a bite."

Teddy didn't know what to do as he flashed his eyes around the room.

"Oh, perfect," said Thomas, taking a deep breath and stabbing his fork into the catfish, hoping to avoid the gumbo as long as he could. After shoveling a heaping mouthful of catfish into his mouth, he smiled and nodded as Roland fixated on his reaction.

"Well?" he asked.

"It tastes wonderful!"

"Oh, excellent," Roland said as he turned his attention to Teddy. "My word, Mr. Bear! You ate all the gumbo already?"

Thomas' eyes grew wide as he stared at the shifty bear.

"Oh, yes, Roland. It was quite tasty. Well done, sir. Now, I will focus on the rest of this delicious meal."

With Roland's attention on Teddy, Thomas peeked under the table. *What did that bear do with the gumbo?*

"Please, Thomas. Try the gumbo," Roland said, startling Thomas to where he sprung up and knocked his head against the edge of the table. "With Mr. Bear being as picky as he is, I'm certain you will enjoy it as well."

"Uhm, right, yes," Thomas said as he looked around.

"Is something wrong?" Roland asked.

"Wrong? No, of course not."

"You really must try it," Teddy said with a huge smile on his face. "I would love to see your face as well."

After taking a deep breath, Thomas put a tiny amount on his fork and raised it up to his mouth.

"No, no, Thomas. To truly enjoy this delicacy, you must get all the different ingredients on your fork at one time."

"Yes, Thomas. That's what I did, and it was well worth it!"

Thomas paused for a moment, hoping for some sort of distraction, like a hurricane.

"There's nothing wrong with Roland's cooking, is there?" Teddy asked, raising his eyebrows.

Roland's smile slowly faded and his head slumped down.

"No. Of course not," Thomas said, shooting Teddy an icy stare.

He shoveled as much of the gumbo onto his fork as he could fit, and in one quick motion, jammed it into his mouth. The unpalatable flavors exploded across his tongue, causing him to squeeze his eyes shut as he slowly chewed the concoction. Teddy watched in delight as Thomas crunched down on something he assumed was a cricket, causing him to turn a pale shade of green. Roland's smile returned as he awaited the review.

"Mmm, excellent," Thomas said through gritted teeth. "And what a unique flavor." He held a finger up as he tried to chew and speak at the same time. Each muscle in his neck flexed while he struggled to suppress his gag reflex and keep the disgusting mixture in. After he finished chewing, he forced himself to swallow the heap of food.

"Well? How was it? What was your favorite part?" Roland asked.

Teddy stared at Thomas with a mischievous smile, his chin resting on his paws to match Roland.

"Wow, well," Thomas said, clearing his throat before grabbing his glass of water and swallowing a big gulp. "I guess the way the crunchiness breaks up the chewiness."

"Oh, I'm so delighted you like it!" Roland said as he tapped his fingers together. "It is so difficult to capture those two consistencies. To you, gentlemen," he said, raising his glass in the air.

Thomas couldn't speak as he raised his glass. All the while, Teddy strained his contorted face to keep from bursting out laughing.

After dinner, the trio retreated to the study, where an overstuffed couch awaited them.

"Mr. Bear, please make certain your paws are mud free. I just cleaned the furniture."

Teddy sneered at Rowland before lifting his feet for inspection. "Is this clean enough, Your Highness?"

"I suppose for a bear of your stature it is. Please, join us."

Teddy grumbled as he climbed up on to the couch.

"Ahh, what an enchanting evening," Roland said as he reached over and grabbed a porcelain teapot. "Thomas, I want to thank you for the delightful company. May I interest you in a spot of tea?"

Teddy raised an eyebrow. "And just what is a 'spot' of tea, exactly?" he asked.

"Sorry. I forget your upbringing, Mr. Bear. Can I offer you a 'cup' of tea?"

"No, thank you, Roland," Thomas blurted out before this went further. "That delicious dinner filled us up."

"I believe I'll have some tea," Teddy said as he took the teapot from Roland.

"Thomas, might I ask, what is your plan of action? The Screech is known throughout the forest as a creature even the bravest travel out of their way to avoid."

"I'm not sure," Thomas said, leaning forward, his head resting in his hands. "Dorian said the Golden Pixie had a way to defeat The Screech. We can't keep running, so we need to find out where she is and partner up with her. The Screech is getting closer each day. We need to end this once and for all."

"Well, you can always build a little place here."

Teddy spit out his tea and turned to Thomas, who leapt up and wiped the bear's face with his napkin before jamming the linen into Teddy's mouth to ensure he didn't say anything obnoxious.

"The Screech has never ventured this far in. I don't think it can survive in the mud," Roland said.

"That's good to hear. I do worry about you being alone out here. If this doesn't work out with the Golden Pixie, we'll consider your option as Plan B."

"Oh, you mustn't worry about me. My family has a long history of defeating dangerous creatures. My bloodline goes all the way back to medieval times. Did you know one of my ancestors was even a knight?"

"Really?" Thomas said, sitting up.

"Oh, yes!"

Roland hopped off his plush chair and pointed to one portrait on the wall. In it stood a tall frog in tarnished silver armor, which bore dings and scrapes from battle. In one hand, he held his helmet, which had a large red plume erupting from the top of it, while in his other hand was a small sword. To Thomas' delight, underneath the painting was the actual sword mounted on the wall.

"This, gentlemen, is Sir Willard. He fought many creatures over in the old land before settling here quite some years ago. As you can see, he wore shining armor and exemplified the bravery of our bloodline. So, you see, I treat The Screech as a minor inconvenience."

"That's amazing! Is that an actual knight's sword?" Thomas asked, his eyes wide.

"It is indeed! My family has displayed it for generations." Roland removed the sword and handed it to Thomas, who took it and swung the blade a few times before thrusting it forward. "It suits you well."

"This is incredible! Imagine all the battles this has seen," Thomas said, inspecting the steel for any dings or marks from combat.

"We could use a fierce warrior such as yourself around here," Roland said, making certain to look away from Teddy in an obvious slight.

"I couldn't think of a nicer place to live," Thomas said, handing the sword back to Roland.

"Then it's settled!" Roland hung the blade back underneath the portrait of Sir Willard. "Since you have a big day tomorrow, let me get you situated for the night."

After grabbing a lantern from a nearby table, Roland escorted the pair to their sleeping chamber at the end of the hallway. He reached up to turn the doorknob and stepped inside, where he placed the lantern on a nightstand.

"Here we are gentlemen."

In the room were two hammocks suspended from the ceiling. The room was small, but offered a nice, safe place for the pair to rest for the night. On a wooden dresser against the wall was a washbowl and pitcher. Behind that was an old mirror that had lost most of its silvering.

"I took the time to fill the pitcher with water when I was preparing dinner. You can use it to clean yourselves up," he said, purposely looking at Teddy.

"This is perfect, Roland. Thank you," Thomas said.

"My pleasure. I will leave you this lantern. If you need anything during the night, please come find me. My room is the first door on the right."

"We will. Goodnight."

As soon as Roland left, Teddy turned to Thomas. "Under no condition will I be moving to this wasteland! I'd sooner take my chances with The Screech."

"Relax. I don't think it will come to that. I believe Dorian. All we have to do is make it to the cider mill and we'll get our answers. Now let's get some sleep."

Thomas lifted Teddy into one of the hammocks. "Imagine how great it would be to be an actual knight. I could take my lance and stab it into The Screech once and for all. It would never bother us again!"

"That would be great. Then we would never have to come out this way again."

Thomas smiled and shook his head. "Goodnight, you grumpy bear," he said, rubbing Teddy's head before turning out the light. "Hey, wait a second! What did you do with the cricket gumbo?"

In the dark, he heard Teddy snickering. "That's my little secret."

In the morning, sunlight beamed through the portholes in the room, shining directly on Teddy's face.

"Ugh," the groggy bear said, squinting before rolling over and burying his head beneath his paws.

Thomas was already awake and tying his blue blanket around his neck. "Come on. We need to get going if we expect to get to the mill before dark."

"I miss my tree."

"Me too. So, the sooner we get this done, the sooner we can go back."

Teddy rolled over and dropped to the floor.

"Should we wake Roland?" Thomas asked.

"No. Let the poor frog, oh, my apologies, 'toad,' let the poor toad sleep," Teddy said as they tiptoed past Roland's door. "Don't worry. I'll leave him a friendly note while you go outside and map out our route."

"Are you sure?"

"Of course. It's the least I can do after he offered his gracious hospitality. I'll meet you out back."

Thomas pulled the map out of his pocket and crept out the door, trying not to wake Roland.

Teddy smiled and took one of the white linen napkins off the table. He opened a window that was closest to the ground, and reaching out, dipped his paw into the mud. With a mischievous smile, he composed his thank you.

Dearest Roland,
Thank you so much for the
accommodations. The cricket gumbo was
as good as your company...

Hope to see you soon.

Regards,
Theodore E. Bear

(P.S. I couldn't find any paper...)
(P.P.S. Or a pen...)

Teddy lay the soiled napkin across the couch cushion and giggled his way out the door.

"What's so funny?" Thomas asked.

"Huh? Oh, nothing. Did you figure out where we're going?"

"Yeah, we have to go northwest. The Screech seems to favor the dirt paths and roads, so we would be smart to stay off them, but I'm not sure we can get there without them. Follow me. We'll take a look."

CHAPTER FIVE

CAMELOT TOWERS

T HE DUO HEADED OUT across the swamp. The day promised to be warm, and the cicadas were already out announcing the hot weather. But it was still early enough to where a thin fog hovered across the muck, making their jump across the slick stones more treacherous. The pair stayed vigilant, vowing to stay dry as they hopscotched across the various stones that were barely visible in the nearly dried-out riverbed. The stench of wet mud filled the air, causing the fussy bear to grumble with each step. Thomas took great joy in watching the balancing act Teddy performed after nearly taking several spills into the slop. Once they reached solid ground, the bear's scowl disappeared, and he presented a rare smile.

"This is more like it," he said, wiping his soiled paws on a clump of leaves and inspecting his fur.

Thomas removed the map and checked it once again. "Okay, so Roland's house is on our right," he said, twisting the map to align it with where they were standing. "Up ahead, on the left, we should come across Camelot Towers. Beyond that will be the apple orchard and then the mill. By my calculations, we should be able to get there well before dark."

After scouting the area ahead, it was just as he suspected. The ground was covered with fallen trees, jagged rocks, and a number of other pitfalls that proved too treacherous to navigate. They would need to use one of the trails. Just off the road, protected by a line of scrub trees, was a dirt path that looked like it hadn't been used in years. Various plants had spread across the clearing, masking the deep holes and ruts that pitted the trail.

"Okay, we're going to have to use this trail. It's in pretty rough shape, so it'll take us longer to get to the mill, but hopefully The Screech will have to move slower too. That might give us time to hear it before it creeps up on us. There is a road over there, which will get us there quicker, but I don't think we should take that chance. What about you?"

"I always like to err on the side of caution," Teddy told him. "It took me long enough to get you out of that tree yesterday. I shudder to think what could've happened if you didn't listen to me."

"It's settled then. We'll go a little deeper into the woods and follow the path the best we can." Thomas looked on either side of the trail. "It's pretty thick with trees and brush over that way, so even if The Screech uses the road, we should be well hidden."

They sidestepped through several thorn bushes and made their way into the thicker part of the forest. The trees on this side of the path had grown close together, and the undergrowth of ferns, weeds, and grass spread wildly between them all. It was the perfect place to stay concealed. Just to be extra cautious, Thomas would look over periodically to make certain they couldn't be spotted from the road. Once they got in deep enough, it wasn't a long hike before the path came to a dead-end at the entrance to the parking area for the playground. Before entering the clearing, Thomas peeked out from behind a tree to make sure it was deserted.

Camelot Towers had been built decades ago when a developer constructed a new neighborhood not far from where they were. Built from rounded timbers, the playground was a series of square interconnected log towers connected by bridges built with sturdy rope and wood planks. To Thomas, it resembled a medieval castle that he and Teddy would often storm, defeating the angry warlord that lived within. When they were finished saving the kingdom, they would escape to the

assortment of slides and swings. After climbing over the wood-timber fence encircling the playground, Thomas removed his school backpack and pulled out an assortment of snacks.

"Excellent idea!" Teddy said. "I'm famished."

"Well, you have your choice of apples, granola bars, or Cheesy Poofs."

"Well, you know what I'm taking," Teddy said as he snatched the bag of Cheesy Poofs from Thomas' hand.

"Alright then. I guess my choice has been made for me."

Thomas and Teddy took their lunch over to the old swings and sat on the faded vinyl seats. Both of them munched away while they lazily kicked their legs back and forth. The serenity of birds chirping in the distance framed the tranquil setting, which was only interrupted by the rusted chains squeaking with each swing. Thomas enjoyed coming here. It had been a long time since he'd been back. Some of his fondest memories were those of his parents bringing him here. They would spend the day playing, his father chasing him across the rope bridges from tower to tower. After that, his mom would push him on the swings right before they sat down and ate their picnic lunch. They'd all sit on the grass, on a red and white checkered blanket, laughing and joking. By the end of the day, his father would have to carry him home as he slept on his shoulder. Thomas knew he'd never have that again. Those days of carefree afternoons were gone. He snapped out of his trance and turned to Teddy, who was busy crunching away.

"Do you miss it?"

"Miss what?" Teddy asked, in mid-chew, smacking his lips.

"Being home."

Teddy stopped munching and thought about it. "I do," he said. "I especially miss waking up in the morning and going out to my porch where I would sip my tea and nibble my cinnamon toast as I looked out from my tree."

Thomas nodded. "You could've stayed behind."

Teddy scowled and looked him in the eyes. "Why would you say that?"

"I don't know. I'm just thinking I took you away without even asking how you felt."

"Well, I stuck with you during the grape juice on the new carpet incident. Why would I abandon you now?"

Thomas nodded. "I know. I guess I'm just —"

"Have you given any thought as to where we go from here? I mean, what are we going to do after we defeat The Screech?"

Thomas thought for a moment.

"I'm not sure. There's always going to be a Screech out there tormenting one thing or another. Maybe we can be their heroes! We can travel the forest, defeating all those who spread tyranny and injustice," Thomas said, standing up, hand on his heart as he stared into the sky.

"So, now you want to be superheroes? What happened to being a knight?"

"I am a knight! It's all the same!"

"Is it though?" Teddy asked. "I mean, one minute we're storming a castle. The next we're flying around fighting crime."

"I never said anything about flying! You — you're really frustrating sometimes, you know that?"

"Aww, come on. I'm just messing around. That sounds like a lot of fun. We should do that."

Thomas sat silent with his forehead scrunched, scowling at the trees. Of course, Teddy couldn't let it go.

"So tell me, Thomas," he said, snickering. "How was the cricket gumbo?"

Thomas sneered at him and turned away. "I don't want to talk about it."

"Was it actually crunchy AND chewy at the same time?"

But there was no response except for the loud crunching of an apple. Teddy couldn't contain his glee as he giggled and searched through his bag of treats for any remaining Cheesy Poofs.

Before he took his next bite of apple, Thomas stopped. "What was that?"

"What was what?" Teddy asked, crunching away as he fixated on the next puff he held in his paw, oblivious to anything else.

Thomas froze, his eyes darting back and forth as he scanned the area. Another crack of a branch caught Teddy's attention. He turned to Thomas, his eyes wide with fear and his mouth covered in orange powder.

CHAPTER SIX

THE WENDIGO

"DOES THIS PLACE EVER end?" Bushner asked, taking a turn down what must've been the tenth trail he had come across.

Spillen stared at her phone. The picture of Thomas' map had several landmarks sketched out, and Spillen was going to make sure they checked them all.

"Yeah, but not until you get to the state line. I come out here often when I need to clear my head. You should try it. There are a lot of good hiking trails."

"Nah, not for me. I'm more of a sit on the couch with a bowl of chips playing video games kind of guy."

Spillen rolled her eyes and smiled.

"What makes you think the kid is out here? Seems pretty spooky."

"You saw the drawings. Plus, like his mother told us, they used to come out here all the time. If he's missing his dad, or feels he has to hide, what better place?"

Bushner raised his eyebrows and shrugged. "I could come up with a hundred right off the top of my head."

"And I'm sure all of them would be back in town. Where, if he was there, I guarantee we would've heard about it by now."

"What if he's not able to walk around?" Bushner asked as he turned to Spillen and raised his eyebrows.

"We're not going to think like that. Thomas is fine. He's just angry and is somewhere blowing off steam."

Spillen stared out the window as the car bounced along the rough road. The trees were beautiful. Their textured bark and bountiful branches captured her focus as they drifted by, creating a perfect refuge for her thoughts. Her mind wandered back to her days in the foster homes. How many times she herself ran away from them, angry, lost. The nights she spent sleeping on the streets, in unlocked cars, trying to escape the people who took her in just for the guaranteed money. She was nothing more to them than a paycheck, but that wasn't always the case. Many families showed themselves to be caring, good-hearted people who hoped to give her a chance. But, by the time she found those homes, the ones she could see herself growing up in, she had been too broken, and time had become too short to change anything. Sometimes, she wished she could find these people and explain her side to them; apologize for the ill-tempered bratty kid she had become. But they probably had already forgiven her. Given her squandered opportunity to some other worthy kid. In the end, she never blamed them for her failed upbringing. How do you reach a kid who lost her parents and didn't want to be found?

"Can't you just imagine the history that took place in these woods?" she muttered, her fist under her chin, resting her head against the window.

"I don't know. All I can think about is how many dead bodies are buried here. Nobody would ever find them."

She turned to Bushner and raised her eyebrow.

"You have a morbid view of life, don't you?"

"Well, look at this place. Paths trailing off everywhere, going God knows where. I'd be shocked if we find our way out of here."

Spillen decided to have some fun. She sat up and locked her door, prompting an odd stare from Bushner. It took everything in her not to smile as she continued to stare out the window.

"You know, there's some crazy story about an ancient creature that roams these woods."

"Here we go," Bushner said, rolling his eyes.

"No, really. You've lived here long enough. Surely, you've heard the rumors. The Native Americans used to tell stories about it all the time. They called this beast the 'Wendigo.' It was said to be a horrific beast with razor sharp fangs that fed on the souls of young children, but when there weren't any of them left to take, the Wendigo would lie in wait for the unsuspecting traveler. This thing would slowly stalk its prey. You'd be out, enjoying a walk or whatever, and, out of nowhere, the Wendigo would attack. Before you could even scream, the Wendigo would feast on your flesh and use your bones to craft a necklace it would wear as a trophy."

Bushner turned to Spillen and smirked. "Really? And just how gullible do you think I am?"

"Well, you said it yourself. I mean, I agree, this place is super creepy. Look, you can research the Wendigo when we get back. It'll prove I'm telling the truth."

She returned to staring out the window, chuckling inside while Bushner stayed silent.

"Imagine what it's like when it gets dark out here? The strange sounds that come out of the trees? An unexplained feeling of cold that sweeps past you? I mean, I can't even imagine what's lurking in the shadows. Plus, it's the perfect time of year for the Wendigo to hunt its prey. The days are getting shorter, so some people lose track of time; wander into strange areas looking for that shortcut to get them back home before it's too dark to see. You know, the legend says that the Wendigo can take many forms, but it favors that of a dragon." Spillen shivered. "I get chills just thinking about it."

Bushner shook his head. "Okay, I get it. Keep looking for the kid, will you?"

She creaked out a smile as she continued looking out the window. She wasn't sure if it had been her story or not, but Bushner was more attentive as his head swiveled about. They came to the end of the trail, where there was an old split-rail fence.

"Hey, we're at the orchard. Should we check out the old cider mill?"

"Yeah. This is one of the places Thomas drew on his map."

The detectives stepped out of the car and were greeted by the subtle scent of apples as they walked past the elder trees.

"It's a shame nobody makes cider here anymore," Spillen said. "Maybe I can buy this place when I retire and get it up and running again."

"Yeah, you do that," Bushner said as they approached the old structure. "Now if you want to talk creepy..."

"I don't know. I think it's got some rustic charm to it."

"You're crazy."

Aside from some missing pieces of slate on the roof, and a few broken windows, the mill itself was in pretty good shape for something its age. It was originally built as an outpost during the French and Indian War, so the exterior walls were thick. Constructed with stacked stone and mortar, it was built to withstand any attacks. There were even escape hatches secreted in the floors and walls. During the turn of the century, a farmer purchased the property and planted the apple trees. Sometime later, he attached a massive wooden waterwheel to the side of the building to help crush the apples, but neither it, nor the mill, had been used for decades.

They stepped through the overgrown weeds surrounding the building and peeked in the windows.

"Nobody's been here in years," Spillen said, wiping the dirt off the glass.

"Thomas?" Bushner called out, but there was no response.

"Hello! Police! Is anyone here?"

There was nothing but silence. They continued searching around the building, but they couldn't find any footprints.

"Let's check inside."

Bushner pushed on the door, but it was jammed shut. Spillen went over to help, and between the two of them, they threw their shoulders against the thick wooden door, forcing it open. Dust spilled down from the beams above them as they entered the mill.

"Police! Is anyone here?"

There was only one large, open room, and it was empty. The air smelled stale and they could taste the dust in the air. Some windows had broken glass, but the jagged edges left behind would've cut anyone to shreds if they tried to come through them.

"Nobody's been in here. Let's go check some of the other places."

The detectives shut the door, which closed much easier than it had opened. Spillen inspected the door and latch.

"He would've never been able to open this by himself. Let's drive over to Camelot Towers. He also marked that on his map, so there's a chance he could've gone that way."

CHAPTER SEVEN

ROXY'S HIDEOUT

T HOMAS AND TEDDY REMAINED frozen as they strained their ears, worried the next sound would be the requiem for their souls. A crack of a nearby branch caused them to jump.

"Quick, we need to go," Thomas said.

He grabbed Teddy by the paw and led him through the playground and into the thick underbrush. As soon as they made their way through the bushes, they sprinted down the narrow trail. Not far behind them, they heard leaves crushing under the quick patter of paws slapping against the ground. The sound grew louder, telling them that whatever was coming was coming quick! Focused on that noise, their attention was diverted when, to their side, they heard the same trampling sound. Thomas didn't know which way to run. Within an instant, he heard a frightening growl before he was tackled to the ground and his backpack ripped away from him.

The force of the strike caused Thomas to tumble forward. Once he stopped rolling, he jumped up and scanned the area until the fierce, cold eyes staring back at him captured his attention. Just ahead, an enormous gray wolf towered over him.

"Teddy, where are you?"

"Well, well Maurice, what do we have here?" The wolf's gruff voice was slow and his words calculated. Each word was chosen with cunning precision as he stared at Thomas.

Teddy pushed the smaller wolf's paw off him and ran over to Thomas, hiding behind his leg.

The two wolves got low and crept closer to the pair.

"We're just trying to get to the cider mill. We don't want any trouble," Thomas said.

The wolves encircled the pair. It was clear who was in charge. Maurice was thin and disheveled, while the other clearly consumed an excess share of the food they gathered. His brawny muscles rippled under his pristine, thick fur.

"And why would you want to go to that place? Nobody has been there for a long time and I'm afraid to say it has fallen into disrepair. It's quite dangerous. Especially for two younglings, such as yourselves. Perhaps we can change your mind."

"We have to go there so we can find the Golden Pixie. She'll help us stop The Screech."

"The Golden Pixie, you say? Hmm. I believe I saw her not too far from here. Just a little while ago. Wasn't that who we saw this morning, Maurice?"

"Huh? No, I don't remember seeing —"

The mighty wolf swung his head to Maurice, baring his teeth and snapping at him. The smaller wolf jumped back, and as if he just finished drinking his weight in espresso, his words jumped from his mouth as he spewed his response. "Oh, right, THIS morning... that's what you said, Tanner, didn't you? Silly me. I was thinking of the other — yes. We did see her this morning. Where exactly was that again?" he asked, blowing the matted fur out of his eyes, revealing a dull expression on his face.

Tanner squeezed his eyes shut and shook his head. "Anyway," he said, presenting a wide, toothy smile, "we can take you to her if you'd like."

"I don't like this," Teddy whispered, his arms wrapped tight around Thomas' leg.

Thomas' first instinct was to flee. However, even though this wolf was massive, he was raised to run down prey, and Thomas' two legs were no match for the four agile pistons of the wolf.

"I don't either," he said to Teddy before turning to the wolves. "That's okay. We have our map, so we're good. But thank you for the offer."

"No, we must insist," Tanner said as the pair came so close, Thomas could feel Tanner's warm breath on the back of his neck as the wolves continued to circle them. "The woods aren't safe for you to be traveling alone."

Maurice chuckled and his eyes sparkled as a sinister smile swept across his face. "Especially with it being so close to lunch and all."

Tanner pushed his muzzle against Thomas' back, prodding him along as Maurice got low and stared at Teddy.

"Okay, sure. Thank you. This will be a great help," Thomas said, grabbing his backpack. After grasping Teddy's paw, they followed Maurice, with Tanner close behind.

"What are we going to do?" Teddy asked.

"I'm not sure. Try to walk slower until I figure something out."

"Not much farther now," Tanner said as they approached a break in the path.

Just as Maurice took his next step, a net sprang up from underneath a patch of leaves and the wolf was whisked up into the air in one quick motion. The fur on Tanner's back stood straight as he growled and turned, hunting for the assailant. Thomas and Teddy froze for a moment while Tanner was distracted.

"Quick! Get on my back!"

Teddy climbed on Thomas' back. As soon as he was secured, Thomas took off, sprinting deeper into the woods.

Tanner turned, ready to pounce on the duo until a rock struck him between the eyes with a loud crack. A stream of blood trickled through his thick fur as he tried to shake off the pain. Before he could react, another rock came hurling at him, striking him in the eye this time. He howled and rubbed his face along the ground before retreating into the darkened woods. Thomas came to an abrupt stop as Tanner charged past him. Out of nowhere, a laugh erupted from the trees high above.

"That'll teach you to mess with my family!"

Teddy slid off Thomas' back and they stood silent, searching for who could've saved them. On a thick branch ahead of them, hidden within the leaves, was a raccoon holding an odd-looking spear. She wore two weighted bandoliers, chock-full of rocks, across her chest. The raccoon scampered down the tree trunk and ran up to Teddy and Thomas.

"We'd better go! That fleabag is more stubborn than me."

"What about him?" Thomas asked, pointing up at the suspended net. All that was visible were Maurice's legs, tangled within the net as he kicked away, trying to free himself.

"What about him?" she said, scoffing before turning and sprinting into the underbrush.

Teddy and Thomas glanced at each other before they ran after her.

A short distance later, they caught up to the stranger just as she darted up the side of an old, majestic maple tree; the largest one around.

"Come on!" she said. "Follow me."

Thomas stared up at the towering tree and shrugged his shoulders.

"Okay, Buddy. Hop on," he said.

Teddy gave him a quizzical stare before climbing up onto his back.

"I don't like this one bit," he said as he unzipped Thomas' backpack and slid himself inside. The only part of him visible were his two eyes peeking out of the bag as Thomas grabbed hold of the first branch.

"She made it look so easy," Thomas said, grunting as he reached for the next limb.

The tiny bear peeked out and glanced down at the ground as Thomas did his best to climb the elder tree. After seeing how high they were, he retreated back into the bag.

"Nope, this is not going to end well."

With the added weight, Thomas was much slower than their new friend, who had already disappeared into the thick canopy. After breaking through the sprawling growth of leaves on the uppermost branches, the pair came across a log cabin built into the tree. The cabin was old, but blended in perfectly with the tree bark. Unless you knew it was there, chances are you would never see it from down below. Wooden shingles covering the roof were peppered with green moss, and the aged timbers making up the exterior walls were cut without removing their outside bark, creating the perfect camouflage. Thick shutters with carved out slits covered the windows. The masked stranger opened the door and ran inside, followed closely by Thomas and Teddy.

"It's all good now. Wolves can't climb."

She removed her waist pack and bandoliers before setting her spear in the corner.

"What is that?" Thomas asked, pointing to the spear.

"Oh, it's my own design," she said, picking up the weapon and spinning it in her hand like a propeller before thrusting the sharpened tip into the wood floor. "I call it a spear-shot. It combines a spear and a slingshot. Comes in quite handy. Especially when someone is trying to have me for dinner. And not in a good way," she said with a wink.

"This thing is amazing!" Thomas said, inspecting her invention.

The blade was made from a hefty piece of flint that was chiseled down and shaped until the point was as sharp as a needle. The wooden shaft was carved from a hard oak that had been worn smooth. Attached to that was a wooden crossbar, forming a lowercase letter 't'. This crossbar was fitted with a thick elastic strap, which had a leather pouch attached. It was here where the stone rested before being launched at its target.

"I'm Thomas, by the way, and this is Mr. Ted —"

"Ted E. Bear. Mr. Bear, or Theodore, to most," he said, pushing his way past Thomas with his paw extended. "But to my close friends, and those who have saved my life, please, call me Teddy." He grabbed her hand and bowed before kissing it.

"Uhm, thanks. Pleasure to meet both of you. My name is Roxanne, but my friends call me Roxy." Roxy pulled her hand away and wiped it on the side of her leg.

"Thank you so much for saving us! I thought we were goners, but then, when I looked up and saw you, I knew we had a chance. You're really fast! All I saw was a blur of a black mask as you jumped from tree limb to tree limb!"

"You need to be fast around here if you want to survive. Those two idiots stole my father from me, so I owe them one. But I don't want to get rid of them too quick. I want to make them suffer. It's turned into a game of cat and mouse with us, so I always try to keep track of where they are." Roxy walked over to a chart on the wall. She grabbed a stick that had the tip charred by fire, which she used to mark an 'X' showing where they just were. "They're not the brightest, but they're fast. Now, let's get you two back on track. Where were you headed?"

"Well, we are trying to track down the Golden Pixie."

There was a single knock against the door, followed a moment later by another one. Roxy did a combat roll over the back of the couch and lurched over, grabbing her spear-shot before inching her way to the door.

"Maybe those two morons learned how to climb after all."

CHAPTER EIGHT

DISCARDED HOPE

S PILLEN AND BUSHNER TURNED into the dusty parking lot of Camelot Towers. Ghostly reminders of childhood exuberance stood sentry just ahead of them. Rusted swings, aged towers, and toppled slides, now stood silent; relics of youthful memories. The sprawling playground had been built in a clearing within Creekside Woods that covered several acres. But that was decades ago, and it had seen better days. Once a popular getaway for families to bring their kids for a picnic and playtime, it was now frequented by hooligans looking to start trouble. Although it was quiet and peaceful during the daylight hours, you didn't want to be around when the sun went down. The darkness and isolation attracted groups of raucous teenagers looking to blow off steam. Spillen stepped out of the car and glanced around.

"I haven't been here in years," she said. "It's sad to see this place like this."

Most of the picnic tables had either been burned or broken apart; the splintered wood being used to build giant bonfires. Some timbers making up the towers were charred from the bored and disenchanted as they tried to set them on fire. The sandbox was full of cigarette butts, and graffiti was sprayed across most of the structures.

"I think it's best to split up. You head over in that direction. I'll go this way and we'll meet by the towers."

"Sounds good," Spillen said.

In case Thomas was scared and hiding, Spillen took a wide sweep into the woods just outside of the clearing. The ground was full of empty beer bottles and cans. She searched for any sign that he'd been here as she made her way to the towers. There was nothing that stood out to her until she got to the play area. Next to the swings, Spillen reached down and picked up a discarded bag of Cheesy Poofs. There were several still in the bag, and a few scattered on the ground. She kneeled down and grabbed one, squeezing it between her fingers. It was still crisp, so it hadn't been on the ground for long. Plus, there was a distinct snap when she broke it in half.

"Hey, Bushner, I need to go to the car and make a call."

Spillen walked back to the parking lot and looked around to make certain nobody was nearby. She got into the car and took out her cellphone.

"Hello, Mrs. Bristol, this is Detective Spillen. No, I'm sorry, we haven't found him yet, but I promise you, we're out looking for him. The reason I called is that I wanted to ask you a question. Does Thomas eat a snack called Cheesy Poofs?" she asked, staring at the package. "He does. Okay, I'll wait."

Bushner got to the car and stood next to Spillen's door. "What's going on?"

"I called Mrs. Bristol. One of Thomas' favorite snacks is Cheesy Poofs," she said, showing Bushner the package. "She's checking to see if there are any bags in her pantry. Hello, yes. Oh, okay. Thank you for checking. No, there's no sign of him yet. I figured he must've brought some food with him when he left, so I wanted to make sure we have whatever information we can get in case we find something that might lead us to him. If you think of anything important, please let me know. Right, you can text or call. Thank you, Mrs. Bristol." She put her phone away and looked at Bushner. "All the bags of Cheesy Poofs she bought the other day are gone."

"You can't be sure this bag was from him."

"No, but they're still crisp, so they're fresh. And it's a school day, so no kids are around. I'd say that's a pretty good sign we're on the right track."

CHAPTER NINE

THE UNEXPECTED GUEST

ROXY STOOD NEXT TO the door, her neck stretched, straining to listen as she waited to see if there were any more knocks on the door — none. She took a deep breath and turned to Thomas.

"If it's those two chuckleheads, I'll do my best to hold them off while you guys run out the back," she said with her spear at the ready, gripped tight in her hand.

She crouched low and reached for the doorknob with her free hand. With a solid grip on the handle, she flung the door open, bellowing out a battle cry as she raised her weapon.

As if suspended in slow motion, Dorian's eyes grew wide and he sluggishly raised his hands up.

"Don't... shoot," he managed to say.

"Dorian! What in tarnation are you doing here?" Roxy said, grabbing the sloth by the arm and yanking him inside. She lowered her spear-shot and propped it up in the corner.

"You invited me to lunch."

Roxy's shoulders dropped, and she frowned. "That was a month ago."

"I had trouble finding your place."

"You've been here before."

"Okay, so it took me longer than I thought."

Thomas and Teddy came out of hiding from another room.

"What are you guys doing here?" Dorian asked, strolling into the living room.

"You all know each other?"

"Yeah," Thomas said. "Hey, Dorian. We ran into these two wolves, Maurice and Tanner. Roxy jumped in and saved us."

"Oh... boy."

"Well, since we're all together, and apparently I still owe Dorian a lunch, can I interest you guys in some food?"

Teddy perked up and rubbed his paws together. "Yes, that would be lovely! I believe Tanner and Maurice scared the last lunch out of me, so I'm starving."

Roxy scrunched her face. "Uhm, okay..."

"Thank you," said Thomas, rolling his eyes. "If it's not too much trouble."

"No trouble at all. I'll be right back," she said, grabbing her spear-shot. After strapping the weapon across her back, she collected two baskets from the kitchen and made her way out the door.

While Roxy was out gathering some food, Thomas explored the cabin, while Teddy collapsed on the couch, dragging a plaid comforter over himself.

"I can't take much more of this," he said, throwing his arm over his eyes and snuggling under the blanket.

"That was an excruciating walk," Dorian said before he settled into an overstuffed recliner. With one leg bent across the armrest and his head dangling over the other, it wasn't long before he too drifted off to sleep.

Thomas took this moment of peace to take a tour of the cabin. The inside was rustic, with its log timbers and wood plank floor, it was built solid. To reinforce the walls, massive oak beams made up the framework of Roxy's home. This was a cabin that could withstand any kind of attack. Plus, since it was so far off the ground, the timber frame home was designed to be inaccessible. Even if someone were to make it all the way to the top of the tree unscathed, they could only approach the cabin from one branch, leaving them off-balanced. Throughout the inside, Roxy had strategic placements for all her weapons. Each window had a station fitted with buckets of rocks and stacks of spears. If necessary, she could rain them down on anyone trying to make their way up the tree.

Thomas made his way into the kitchen. Grabbing a glass, he walked over to the sink. There was a hand pump attached to the counter for water.

"Oh, cool!"

After several pumps of the handle, water dripped from the spout before gushing into the sink. He filled his glass and continued admiring the work Roxy put into the place. Gingham curtains and pictures of her family softened the drab, rustic space. Ceramic and glass vases burst with fresh flowers, filling the room with a fragrant scent. A large, stone stacked fireplace in the center of the room complimented the cozy setting.

"This place must get toasty in the winter," Thomas said.

Down the hall, there were two bedrooms, a bathroom, and beyond that was an oddly placed, fortified door. With its thick planks and iron braces, the door looked as though it should be protecting a castle. After heaving up the metal latch, Thomas pulled the door open. Beyond was a small opening carved into the tree. The only thing in this space was a brass pole that disappeared down into the darkened, hollowed-out tree trunk.

"Wow! Roxy thought of everything." he said as he tried to see the bottom. "A fireman's pole for a quick escape."

"That's one of my favorite things," Roxy said, startling Thomas.

"I'm sorry. I hope you don't mind me snooping around, but this place is so great!"

"No, I don't mind at all. Fortunately, I haven't had to use the pole to escape." She walked up close to Thomas and put her hand to the side of her mouth. "However, truth be told, I use it more often than not; but just for fun."

Thomas laughed.

"How could you not?"

"I got us some good eats. Should we wake those two?"

As soon as Roxy set some plates on to the table, Dorian's droopy eyes opened. "Is it time to eat?"

Teddy was a little more difficult to wake and was rather unpleasant when he did. With his brow furrowed, he dragged himself over to the table and plopped down onto a chair without a word.

"Here, let me help you," Thomas said, grabbing the baskets full of food Roxy gathered.

"I got lucky and found some honey," she said, pulling a jar out of the basket. Filled to the brim of the glass were hefty chunks of honeycomb, engorged with sweet honey. The golden liquid pooled at the bottom of the jar as it drizzled out from the wax. "This will go great with the bread I made yesterday." She pulled a loaf from the oven. "I warmed it up a bit. Nothing better than fresh, warm bread. In case honey isn't your thing, I made fresh raspberry preserves and grape jam."

She walked over to the pantry and collected several jars from the cabinets, setting them on the table.

"Aside from that, I found some other fresh berries, and there were still apples from the old trees near the mill."

"Are you talking about the old cider mill?"

"Yeah. It's not too far from here. Why?"

"That's where we were headed before Tanner and Maurice stopped us. Last we heard, the Golden Pixie was camped out there."

"Well, I can't say if she was or not, but I didn't see anyone else out in the orchards other than me. Maybe she was in the mill itself. Why are you looking for her?"

"We want to see if she can help us destroy The Screech."

"The Screech? What is that?" Roxy asked.

"It's this gigantic monster that roams the woods and has been chasing us. The Golden Pixie is the only one strong enough to defeat it."

"Really? I've lived here all my life and have never heard of this thing."

"Well, it mostly sticks to the paths and trails when it hunts. Dorian knows about it."

"Huh?" Dorian asked with a mouth full of food.

"Nothing," Roxy said, rolling her eyes. "Just go back to what you were doing. So, Thomas, what exactly does this thing look like?"

"I haven't seen it up close. We've been too busy running away from it. But what I have seen is terrifying! It looks like a dragon, of sorts. It's about ten feet tall and has cold, round, dead eyes with no pupils. Sometimes, when it's angry, its eyes will turn bright red! It has gray skin that's spotted with patches of brown. But Dorian said the patches are just rusted armor that it wears to protect itself. The Screech claimed the shields as trophies after it defeated and ate all the knights who tried to stop it. There are so many shields on it that it clanks every time it attacks!"

"Geez! And I thought Tanner and Maurice were bad news. Have you two seen it up close?" she said, looking over at Teddy and Dorian.

But they were too busy shoveling food into their mouths to pay attention to what Roxy and Thomas were discussing.

"Don't you want any honey, Mr. Bear?"

Teddy's face scrunched up.

"Yech. Can't stand that sticky mess. Do you know how long it takes to get honey out of fur?"

"A bear that doesn't enjoy honey... Now I've heard it all."

"More for me," Dorian said, sticking his long claws into the jar full of golden liquid and licking it from his hands. "Delicious!"

"Well, when we're done with lunch, I can take you over to the mill if you'd like. That way, if this 'Screech' shows up again, you've got an extra set of hands to fight back."

"That would be great! Thank you."

After lunch, Teddy leaned back in his chair and rubbed his swollen stomach.

"That was delicious. I'm so full. Is it naptime now?"

"No. We really need to get going before it gets dark."

"Well, if you two are ready, we can head out. Dorian, you might as well stay here. Chances are I'll be back before you even make it out the door."

Dorian frowned. "Fair enough. I'll just take a quick nap while you're gone."

"So, boys, we have two options. Either we climb down the tree, or we can slide down the pole."

"Thomas' eyes lit up. "The pole! I vote for the pole!"

"Pole? What pole?" Teddy asked.

"You'll love it!" said Thomas as he grabbed Teddy and darted for the door. Flinging it open, he threw Teddy on his back before the bear had a chance to protest. The last thing he heard was Teddy pleading with him to hold on for a minute before Thomas jumped onto the pole and rocketed to the bottom of the tree. The whole way down, Teddy screamed in his ear, praying for it to end. Thomas couldn't control his laughter. By the time they made it to the bottom, Teddy had worked his way into Thomas' backpack, where he shook uncontrollably.

Thomas set the bag down and peeked into the opening. Teddy was hunched over, his head buried in his arms.

"Don't you ever do that to me again! What were you thinking?"

"I was thinking about cricket gumbo," he said, sneering at Teddy, who had nothing further to say about the matter.

"Whoa! I forgot how much fun that was!" Roxy said, as she hit the ground and worked her way through the thorny thickets protecting the hidden opening. "I could do that all day. Okay, you guys ready?"

"Yep. Do you think we need to worry about Tanner and Maurice?"

"Nah. I checked earlier and Maurice is still stuck in my net. Once Tanner finds him, it'll take him at least until tomorrow to gnaw through the rope and get him down."

Roxy used her spear-shot for a walking stick as the trio headed down the narrow trail. High above, the sun speckled through the thick canopy, and the birds chirped away as they darted in and out of the branches.

"It's so peaceful here," Thomas said, looking up into the trees.

"Yeah, for now," Teddy said. "Perhaps you've forgotten we have two wolves angry at us. Plus, we still have The Screech hunting for us. I'm sure it's out there, ready to pounce on us at any moment."

"You couldn't have picked a better place to live," Thomas said.

"I think so. Where do you guys live?" Roxy asked.

Thomas and Teddy looked at each other.

"Usually in a hollowed-out tree next to the school," Teddy said.

"Usually? Was there someplace before that?"

Thomas stopped and stared at the ground. "We were living with my mother, but not anymore."

"Did something happen to her?"

"No. Nothing like that. She, well, she threatened to take Teddy away from me."

"Why would she do that?"

Thomas raised his eyebrows. "It's my fault. I was causing problems and almost got kicked out of school."

"Oh," Roxy said, not wanting to push the issue.

"I miss him. She doesn't get it," Thomas muttered.

"Who?"

"My dad. He was my best friend."

Teddy put his paw on Thomas' shoulder.

"I'm so sorry," Roxy said. "What happened to him?"

Thomas sat down on a nearby boulder. "He was in the army and had to go overseas. My mom never told me what happened. She's probably trying to protect me or something. All I know is he was in some major battle in a small village. There was some kid over there, and my father tried to protect him."

Nobody said anything for some time.

"She doesn't understand. Teddy is everything to me now. When she tried to take him away from me, well — anyway, I couldn't let that happen. I've lost too much, and she doesn't get it."

Roxy stabbed the spear tip into the ground and sat next to Thomas. "Out of all people, I think she gets it the most."

Thomas scowled at her. *What makes you think you know everything?* He thought.

"Look. She's going through the same thing you are, but she needs to stay strong so she can be there for you. Everything you're going through, she's going through the same thing. Your dad was probably her best friend, too. She was probably like me when I lost my dad. All I wanted to do was curl up and cry. I'm sure she wants to do that as well, but she has to be your mom and make sure you're okay."

Roxy stood up and looked Thomas in the eyes.

"After I lost my family, I was left all alone. Sure, you have Teddy. But don't lose anyone else."

Thomas rubbed his sleeve across his tear-filled eyes. Before standing up, he drew in a deep breath. "We should keep moving."

CHAPTER TEN

FORT RIVERSIDE

WITH LITTLE SUNLIGHT ABLE to break through the dense canopy, the surrounding ground in this part of Creekside never fully dried between rain storms. Thus, traveling with a fastidious bear promised to be more challenging than usual. Since Thomas wanted to avoid the wrath of a soiled bear, he carried Teddy most of the way; this was quite agreeable for his furry companion, who relished being pampered. After trudging through the spongy soil, the towering trees grew sparse. Once crammed with an abundance of maple, elm, and pine trees, the group had stepped into an expansive swath of land, cleared decades ago by a farmer who went to great lengths to plant an apple orchard. As they approached their destination, the sweet scent of apples filled their nostrils as the breeze blew past the fruit dangling from nearby branches.

"I'm seeing more apple trees," Thomas said.

"Yup. We're getting close. This is the outskirts of the mill."

The path they had been on wiggled its way through the abandoned orchard. It was clear to see the field hadn't been tended to for years. Weeds grew rampant in-between the sagging, overburdened trees as lush apples still filled the branches of the aged timber. So bountiful was the fruit, that many apples were crowded off the trees and lay scattered along the ground. Back in the early days, when this portion of land was cleared, the farmer started with only a handful of trees. The rich soil from the nearby river made this an ideal place for his crop. He worked the orchard for decades before his death. After that, it remained in the same family for several generations. Over the following years, more scrub trees were cleared, and the orchard grew in size as the demand for apples increased. When Prohibition came, they planted more and more apple trees after the mill began producing hard cider. Since it was hidden deep in the forest, it remained a secret and one of the few orchards not burnt to the ground during the Temperance Movement. Another advantage to its proximity along the river was the convenience of transporting the cider along the trails to waiting boats. This helped the mill with a stealthy delivery system for its illegal drink. Each time a rival orchard was destroyed, the family's business blossomed. Once Prohibition ended, so did the overwhelming demand for hard cider. When most of the family passed, the remaining members had no interest in running the orchard. They took their money and abandoned the mill. Over time, it fell into disrepair and was forsaken.

"I'm not sure we should stay on the path." Teddy said, his head on a swivel as he watched for trouble.

Thomas looked around. "We haven't heard from The Screech for a long time. So, I think we're safe."

The closer they got to the mill, the more apple trees popped up until they were enveloped by them. Hundreds of trees, all arranged in neat rows, peppered the landscape for as far as they could see.

"The mill isn't much further now," Roxy said, plucking an apple from a tree and biting into it.

Over the crest of a hill, they saw the worn slate roof of the cider mill. In the past, you'd be able to hear the water in the stream rushing past, turning the massive wheel on the side of the building. But, as with the river where Roland lived, the creek feeding the mill had dried up long ago.

"I don't think she's here," Roxy said, with her ear pressed up against the door, listening intently.

She struggled to turn the rusted iron ring and opened the door, which moaned with age. Since there were no noises inside, the trio popped their heads in and took a peek. Thomas thought the mill was scary enough in the daytime. Now, looking up at the menacing building, he could only imagine what it was like in the dead of night. They stepped into the broad space of the room. Its wide wooden plank floor was covered in dust, and wispy strands of cobwebs clung to the windows.

"Somebody's been here," Roxy said, examining the footprints in the dust.

"Could it have been the Golden Pixie?" Teddy asked.

"I doubt it," Thomas said. "There's more than one set of prints here. They're way too big for her."

"Yeah. Plus, she flies most of the time," Roxy said. "Well, it seems like whoever it was is long gone. Should we get settled in and wait for her here?"

Wind howled through the broken glass. The same gusts pushed the paddles on the waterwheel, forcing the wheel to turn with a high-pitched squeak that was unnervingly similar to The Screech's howl. Some thunder rumbled in the distance, causing Teddy and Thomas to jump when a flash of lightning sent shadows scattering through the room. Roxy looked outside. A massive black cloud swept its way across the sky as the icy wind blew harder.

"It looks like it's gonna get real nasty soon. We should definitely stay inside."

75

"Yeah, I don't like that idea," Thomas said, backing away.

"Well, I'm staying," Teddy said. "My fur has suffered enough on this so-called adventure."

"Is it safe to be here?" Thomas asked.

Roxy stomped on several portions of the floor. "It seems safe enough," she said, even though the wood planking next to the windows had rotted away from years of rain streaming in.

Along the wall, where the waterwheel connected, was an old stone cider press. The massive millstone was attached to a series of rusted metal gears which once worked in unison to move the wheel.

"This is how they made the cider back in the day," Roxy said, walking over to it. "My grandpa told me all about it. They would pile the apples into this circular trough. Then, after flipping some lever, the waterwheel outside would spin, which would turn these gears and make this big stone wheel move. The wheel crushed the apples, and the juice came out here."

She ran her hand along the channel in the stone base that led to a hole with a small groove carved into the stone.

"Come here and take a whiff of this. This is where the cider funneled out. Mmm, you can still smell the cider on the stone."

Thomas closed his eyes and breathed in. Even after all these years, the aroma was sweet.

"Teddy, come on over. Try it."

"That's okay. Hey, how long do you think we should wait?" Teddy asked, fumbling with his hands as he glanced around.

"I don't know. Roland said someone saw the Golden Pixie here, but they didn't say if she lived here, or just stopped by every now and then. By the looks of the place, I doubt she lives here."

Thomas walked around the space, searching for any clues where she might be.

"You can go if you want, Roxy. Teddy and I will wait to see if she comes around."

"Nah. The storm is about to split open the sky. I'll wait it out here with you guys, then head back when it passes."

Roxy walked over to a small stone fireplace in the far corner of the room. "We might as well make a fire to stay warm. Plus, it'll give us some light."

The three of them searched outside and gathered up some old branches before the rain soaked them. After lugging the wood inside, they made a bed of dried grass and leaves in the fireplace. Roxy arranged the logs in a triangle shape on top of the grass before pulling out a knife and stone from her bag.

"What's that for?" Thomas asked.

Roxy looked at the two items. "To make a fire. Haven't you ever started a fire this way?"

"No. When we would go camping, my father used a lighter. He told me he would show me another way when he got back from overseas, but —"

Roxy patted him on the shoulder. "I've got this. What we have here is a flint stone. You can tell because it is black and gray, and has a certain shine to it," she said, showing Thomas the different striations. "I'm gonna take a small piece of cloth and put it next to our wood in the fireplace. Then, taking my knife, I strike the blade against the rock and..."

When she did this, sparks jumped out, causing Teddy to duck for cover.

"Uhm, just make sure you light the wood and not me, please."

Roxy laughed. "No worries, Mr. Bear." She did this a few more times until a flame grew from the cloth. After piling some loose grass on it, the flames grew larger. Once she was satisfied it would stay lit, she slid the cloth into the pile of grass under the wood kindling. Before long, a roaring fire was burning in the fireplace.

"This is nice," Thomas said as the room filled with a soft, warm glow.

"I brought some water, but I'm sorry to say I don't have any food with me. I can run out there and search for some."

A large rumble of thunder shook the mill as the rain came down, pelting the windows with massive drops. Thomas peeked out, wide-eyed.

"I don't think that would be a good idea. Plus, I have some snacks left in my backpack."

Thomas unzipped the large pocket and spread out the food.

"Oh, this is going to be a treat for you!" Teddy told Roxy as he scurried over to Thomas on his knees, his eyes wide in anticipation.

"What's got that bear all worked up?"

"You'll see," said Thomas as he pulled out several bags of Cheesy Poofs.

Teddy snatched one from the pile and sprinted over to the fireplace.

"Here's a bag for you, Roxy. Watch it carefully. He's been known to steal another person's Cheesy Poofs. And he does it with no shame at all. Oh, and here's an apple."

"What exactly is this?" she asked, scrunching her face as she examined the package of treats.

"Well, they're called Cheesy Poofs, but Teddy calls them, 'poofies.' Basically, they are crunchy, cheesy, sticks that have been puffed up with air."

Roxy stared at the package, paying special attention to the image on the front.

"Do they grow like this?"

"Uhm, no. They're kind of made in a factory. A big machine spits them out and bags them up."

"Are they organic?"

Thomas laughed. "Not even a little. I think the package has more nutrition in it than they do. But they taste good."

Roxy shrugged her shoulders and headed over to the fireplace. She plopped down next to Teddy, who had his face buried in the bag.

"Are you okay?"

Teddy pulled his face back, his eyes half-closed in delight, and his nose covered in orange dust. "I'm good," he said, almost dreamlike. "How are you?"

His mouth dropped when he saw the bag in her hand.

"Do you know if there are any more?" he asked, licking the cheesy dust from his lips and looking over at Thomas.

"I think so," she said, glancing over her shoulder.

As soon as she turned back, Teddy had his face inches from her bag.

"Boy, you really like these things, don't you?"

"Yes!" he said, jumping up and scurrying over to Thomas. A short time later, he came back to where Roxy was sitting with his feet dragging. "There aren't any more for tonight," he said, plopping down to the ground.

"Oh. Uhm, do you want mine?"

"I was told I couldn't have yours and not to ask," he said, taking a bite out of the apple in his hand before crossing his arms and looking away.

Roxy opened her bag and put her face near the opening, taking a few quick sniffs. Raising her eyebrows, she pulled out one of the puffed cheese sticks. As soon as she crunched down on it, Teddy's ears perked up, but he refused to look. But as Roxy chewed her treat, Teddy couldn't help but to peek. Roxy's face contorted into a blend of furrowed eyebrows and pursed lips as she continued to chew.

"Well, that's kind of interesting, I guess. But I can't taste any cheese."

Teddy scooted over and crossed his legs. "You have to chew slowly and savor the flavor." He took one out of Roxy's bag and placed it in his mouth, lying it gently across his tongue. As his mouth slowly closed, a smile spread across his face. He looked up, closed his eyes, and waved his hand in the air as though he was drawing in any flavor trying to escape. "Feel the way the powder coats your tongue; listen to the crunch. I'm telling you, this is pure heaven."

"Right..." she said, widening her eyes and raising her eyebrows. She handed Teddy the package. "Perhaps you would enjoy these much more than I could. Why don't we trade?"

"Deal!" Teddy shoved the apple into her chest and snatched the bag from her hand.

Thomas joined them and stared at Roxy, who now had two apples, and Teddy, who was feverishly chowing down on Roxy's bag of Cheesy Poofs. He scowled at the bear.

"It was her idea," Teddy mumbled with a mouthful of orange mush. "I swear!"

Sheets of rain poured down from the sky. Relentless, it pummeled the tiny shelter with such force, it sounded like a freight train rumbling by. With the wind blowing in all directions, rain came in through the broken windows, forcing the trio to huddle around the fire. As they enjoyed their meal, a subtle creak captured their attention. They stopped eating and stared at each other.

"Did you hear that?" Thomas asked.

They all listened intently. Another squeak caused them to stiffen up.

"There it is again."

CHAPTER ELEVEN

THE ESCAPE

R OXY GRABBED HER SPEAR-SHOT as the trio scrambled for cover. They could barely hear anything other than the rain beating down against the roof. Each flash of lightning caused creepy shadows to manifest before them. While they waited, the rusted doorknob slowly twisted. Roxy jumped to her feet and pulled her arm back as she prepared to launch her spear. When the door flung open, a flash of lightning highlighted a tall silhouette in the center of the opening. Scared, Teddy grabbed on to Roxy at the precise moment she threw her spear, which missed its target and embedded itself deep into the doorframe.

"What... the... heck?" a lethargic voice struggled to say.

The shadowed figure stepped into the light.

"Dorian! Why are you here? I nearly killed you. Weren't you going to stay behind?"

The sloth slowly turned and stared at the spear, which was mere inches from his head. His jaw dropped. "That's twice now you've tried to kill me."

"What are you doing here?" Roxy asked.

"The storm scared me."

"Well, get in here."

"No. You scare me."

"Don't be ridiculous," Roxy said, heading to the door and grabbing his arm.

Off in the distance, in the storm's gloominess, two red eyes pierced through the dark.

"It's The Screech!"

Thomas and Teddy ran to the door. Their eyes grew wide as they saw the red glow. Nothing happened for a moment, until without warning, The Screech growled at them and charged. It squealed excitedly as it sped toward the mill, its eyes glowing bright with excitement. The noises it made sent a shiver through Thomas' body. The closer it got, the louder it howled.

Roxy yanked Dorian in and wriggled her spear free. Just before The Screech pounced on them, Roxy slammed the door shut. She ran over and grabbed a hefty timber that was propped up in the corner, covered in cobwebs. Her arms strained as she tried to drag it over to the door. Thomas rushed over and helped her wedge the lumber into the rusted barricade brackets that were bolted into the walls on either side of the door.

"What are we going to do?"

"I'm not sure this old board will keep The Screech out for long," Roxy said, searching for something stronger to brace against the door.

As they scattered to check the room, there was an enormous crash against the door; then another.

"It's trying to get in. We need to get out of here!"

With each crash, the board flexed, tiny splinters of wood splitting away from it as dust drifted to the floor from the rotted timber.

"That board is getting ready to snap!" she said.

"Over here," Dorian sleepily said.

Dorian was suspended off the ground, his feet pressed up against a small trapdoor in the wall next to the water wheel. He jerked on the handle with both hands, but it didn't budge. The others ran over and pulled him off, trying to help him clear the opening, but the years of it being wet warped the wood.

"It's no use! The door is swelled tight into the doorframe," Roxy said. Her face twisted as she struggled to yank on the handle.

A loud crack warned the group The Screech was about to break through. Roxy grabbed some rope from her backpack and strung the line through the handle of the trapdoor.

"All of us need to pull!"

The four of them grabbed hold of the rope.

"On the count of three. One, two, THREE!"

With that, they all yanked on the rope, which caused the little door to fling open with a deafening squeak.

"It's too small for all of us to fit!" Roxy said. "We have to jump one at a time."

As soon as it was clear, each of them launched themselves through the tiny opening as Roxy gathered up the rope. The moment she finished tucking the rope into her hip pouch, the door fractured apart with a shattering crash. Dozens of pieces of wood splintered and exploded into the room. Before The Screech grabbed her, Roxy dove through the opening and splashed down into the muddied creek bed, where the rest of the group waited. Just as they shook the mud off, a loud roar echoed through the darkness.

"The Screech made it in! Hurry! Let's go!" she said.

They scrambled out of the damp soil and sprinted into the orchard. But Dorian, as a sloth often does, was falling behind as he struggled to keep up.

The storm was brutal! The rain whipped sideways as the wind scattered it around. Each drop felt like a bee sting. Hardly able to see through it all, their escape slowed as lightning crashed overhead and the wind blustered through the woods. Even though they weren't moving fast,

Dorian was moving even slower. With the next flash of lightning, Thomas saw something in the shadows that could help.

"Hey! There's an old apple cart there, next to that tree." Thomas said, screaming to be heard over the howling gusts. "Let's throw Dorian in that!"

After tossing a contorted Dorian into the wagon, Thomas swept his rain-soaked hair from his eyes, grabbed the handles, and took off running.

"Come on! Hurry!" Teddy yelled.

Looking back, they spotted the two devilish eyes bouncing toward them in the distance, smoke billowing from The Screech's mouth.

"Keep running! We can blend in among the trees." Roxy said.

They darted through the orchard, heading away from the path where they knew The Screech couldn't follow. When they finally reached the outskirts of the property, they entered the woods and weaved their way deep into the trees. As the roars of the beast grew fainter, the storm began to let up.

"I think we're far enough away now," Thomas said, peeking through the thick brush.

He stepped back, hunched over with his hands on his knees, trying to catch his breath. "We need to find a place to rest for the night."

"Sounds good. The trail is pretty far away. I can build us some shelter and we can camp out here for the night," Roxy said, panting. "If y'all can scavenge around for some thick, straight branches and bring them back here, I can build us a lean-to."

The group scoured the forest and collected as many branches as they could carry. By the time they dragged the wood back, Roxy had already cleared a spot and covered the ground with as many dry leaves as she could find.

"Oh, perfect," she said as she sorted the branches and built the structure. "Sorry, I couldn't make the ground more comfortable. The rain soaked everything."

"I'm sure it will be better than sleeping in the mud," Thomas said. "Thank you."

The storm had caused the temperature to drop, and each of them was drenched. Thomas' clothes clung to him like a second skin. Wet and cold, they huddled together to get warm. It wasn't long before Roxy had stacked the branches tight together and had the lean-to finished. Once she gave the okay, they all gathered together close. With The Screech hunting for them nearby, they didn't want to build a fire and risk the flames giving away their position. Even without it, the lean-to kept them warm and dry. Not only that, it also blended in with the surrounding woods, so even if The Screech ventured off the path, it would have trouble finding them. This night had been excruciating, and it wasn't long before the group drifted off to sleep. They settled into their restful slumber until the snap of a branch caused Thomas to stir.

Chapter Twelve

THE FORBIDDEN WOODS

S EVERAL ACORNS DROPPED FROM high above and bounced off the roof of the lean-to, awakening the tiny blue bear. Thin strands of morning sunlight filtered through the trees and into his eyes as he tried to cover his head, but the pelting of nuts continued.

"It better not be those stupid squirrels," he grumbled.

Through heavy eyes, Teddy rolled over and threw his arm across Thomas, but it fell flat onto his discarded backpack. Teddy shot up when he realized he was alone!

Where did they go?

To the side of Thomas' backpack, Roxy's gear was stacked where she had left it, including her spear-shot.

"They would never go anywhere without these, unless they've gone to grab some food." He looked around and then a thought popped into his head. "But what if they didn't go for breakfast?"

Teddy grabbed Roxy's spear-shot and huddled himself in the corner of the lean-to as he waited for his friends to return. Every sudden noise caused him to jump as he gripped Roxy's weapon tighter. He crawled over and peeked his head out of the lean-to.

"Nothing," he said as he paced. "Where could they be? What if they're in trouble?"

He climbed to the top of the shelter and scanned the area.

"What am I going to do?" he asked, chewing the fur on the end of his paw. "I need to go find them. That's what they would do if I was missing."

After strapping on Thomas' backpack, which was almost as tall as he was, he grabbed Roxy's spear-shot and draped her bandoliers over his shoulders. Overloaded with his friend's belongings, he searched along the ground for some kind of clue to show him what direction they went. All around the lean-to were footprints, but they were so mashed together in the mud, it was difficult to determine which way they headed. After much effort, he found a section of ground that had footprints disappearing off into the distance.

"That must be the direction."

He stumbled through the woods, dragging the gear with him. With the backpack on him, Roxy's hip bag around his neck, the spear-shot, and the bandoliers, the small bear had to stop often just to readjust his load.

"This stuff is so heavy," he said, bent over, trudging along the best he could. With each rest he took, he listened intently for some sign that his friends were okay. He hoped they would call out, giving him an idea of where they were or that they were okay, but there was nothing reassuring him. He took a deep breath and clanked along with the gear in tow.

"Wait a minute. I can lose some of these rocks she has in her bandoliers. That would take a lot of the weight off."

He set everything down and removed the first stone, but stopped.

"What if I get in trouble and need them?" He stared at the rock in his hand and tucked it back into the pocket on the strap. "Well, I certainly don't need ALL of them. I can just leave a couple in."

He pulled out another stone, again standing silent as he stared at it. This went on for a while as he wasted a fair amount of time going back and forth, arguing with himself before throwing the stone in frustration.

"Ugh! What is wrong with me? Just make a decision!" He paced for a moment. "What would Thomas do?" Without any further hesitation, he picked up one bandolier and removed the stones, leaving the other loaded. "There!" he said, before rearranging all the gear and continuing on.

It wasn't long before the little bear approached a portion of woods that screamed for you to stay away. A place long forgotten. Abandoned by the sunlight, by the wind. Those who paid close attention would catch a glimpse of something that may give them trepidation to travel further. Under the scrub brush, hidden from years of uncontrolled growth, was an aged barbed wire fence. With rusted metal barbs and rotted wooden posts, what's left of the fence is more of a relic than it is anything else. Albeit, concerning enough on its own, it was the discarded wooden sign lying near the fence that caused Teddy dread. The faded letters cast an ominous warning; STAY OUT!

It has long been speculated whether this fence was placed by a farmer during one of the first settlements; strung along for miles, protecting his herd. Or perhaps it was from one of the many bootleggers, who did whatever they could to protect their illicit enterprises. Either way, it served its function for many decades, and even though the fence had outlived its usefulness, people entering this section should take heed, remain cautious, for what lies in wait is more dangerous than the sign lets on.

Now, as Teddy stood silent, shaking, he wondered if the fence was put there to keep intruders out, or to keep something in. A once proud, determined bear had now been overcome with dread and despair as he stood before the entrance to this ominous world. It was clear to see the difference between the two sections of terrain. As if someone took a gigantic paintbrush and covered the land before him in a swath of gray and black paint, the woods seemed dead, and that's exactly what he didn't want to be. There were no paths leading into this darkness; just trampled down growth, which his friends must've done when they entered. But why come here? What was the reason for this? Had they somehow lost their minds? Did the Golden Pixie lead them away, or was this the resting place for The Screech? A place where that hideous beast brought all of its prey before it devoured them.

"Hello? Thomas? Is anyone out there?" Teddy half-heartedly called out. As though his feet would be burned by the soil on the other side of the fence, Teddy paced along the edge of the darkened woods, trying to figure out his next move. The foreboding shadows loomed over him. "Maybe they're back at the campsite," he said, trying to convince himself to return and wait for them there, but he couldn't.

Then, through the muted, blanched landscape, an out-of-place bright orange color grabbed his attention. Teddy knew this color. He took a deep breath and slipped through the fence and into the shadowed, dank space. With the spear-shot at the ready, he strode up to the anomalous marker that dared to challenge its drab surroundings. Just as he suspected. It was a discarded Cheesy Poofs bag, dangling from a thorn branch.

"They came this way!"

Before he could change his mind, he pushed his commonsense aside and crept his way through the trees. Every branch he moved was dead and cracked in half. There was nothing here that brought comfort, that breathed life. Between the crunching of the dried up leaves, and the snapping of branches, Teddy feared whatever was out here would certainly know he was coming. After struggling to remain stealthy, he ventured upon a ravine that dipped down into the forest. A large hill on the other side blocked him from seeing what was beyond. All the plants here remained lifeless as well. Even the stream that at one time cut its way through the landscape had long since dried up.

"This place is so depressing," he said as he scampered down into the gully and up the other side. Before he reached the peak, he dropped all the gear except for the spear-shot. "That stuff is making too much noise." he said, now feeling ten times lighter.

Just over the ridge was a clearing, where an outlying of large boulders formed a semi-circle. And within this circle, wrapped up in a net next to a rotting tree, were Thomas and Dorian.

"That's Roxy's net! But why would she trap them?"

He looked around, making sure it was clear, and just as he started down the hill to free his friends, he spotted Maurice dragging a log out of the tree line. Teddy ducked behind a thick oak and watched as the wolf opened his mouth and dropped the log on a pile of wood underneath a rotisserie. And tied to that rotisserie was a lifeless Roxy!

"That's enough wood," Tanner said as he strode out from an opening under the rocks. He looked different. Thanks to his last run in with Roxy, he was now forced to wear an eye patch. "We'll be eating like kings today, my friend."

Through all of this, Roxy still hadn't moved.

"Should I start the fire now, Tanner?"

"Why not? We can have an early lunch. That'll give us time to decide who, I'm sorry, what to have for dinner."

Maurice snickered. "Good one, Tanner!"

The enormous wolf strode up to Roxy and lifted her up by the scruff of her neck. "You weren't so tough without your silly stick, were you?" he said, before releasing her head, which slumped down. "Your father wasn't so tough, either."

"Yeah, he wasn't tough at all; he was nice and tender," Maurice said, licking his lips. "You see what I did there with my word play, Tanner?"

"Yes, Maurice. You're quite the wordsmith. Now get the fire started. I'm famished."

Teddy threw his back against the tree, his mouth dropped open as he struggled to breathe. "What am I going to do? What can I do? I'm just a small bear." He peeked from around the tree and saw Maurice blowing on a clump of dried weeds, which began smoking. "He's almost got it lit. I have to do something fast."

Teddy surveyed the area as he tried to come up with a plan. One that would save his friends and not get himself killed. Up a small earthen incline, on top of Tanner's den, was a wall of rocks which were stacked in order to stop any fallen trees from rolling down the hillside and destroying their home. It was clear to see why they had done this. Several large timbers had already fallen, their crushing weight barely being held back against the stones. Teddy grabbed the spear-shot and crawled away from behind the tree. His stealthy approach seemed to take forever as he struggled to avoid the crack of branches or rustling any leaves. After the spear tapped the side of a nearby tree, Tanner paused and stuck his nose high in the air.

"Is something wrong?" Maurice asked.

Tanner thought for a moment. "No. Just get the fire ready and be quick about it."

Once the wolves returned to their tasks, Teddy stood and scrambled over to the stone wall on top of the den. In the distance, he heard the crackle of Maurice's fire as the flames grew.

"I can use this as cover to stage my assault," he said with his chest puffed. "Dang it! I left Roxy's bandolier back there." He scouted around for some stones to use in his attack. After he collected several, he placed one in the leather pouch of the spear-shot. Cautiously, he peeked over the top of the boulders, doing his best to steady the weapon as he took aim. With all his strength, he pulled back on the elastic band, but the tension was too strong and he lost his grip. The rubber snapped back and stung his paw! Teddy's face twisted with pain as he tried to mask his urgency to scream out. But that wasn't his only challenge. The rock that he launched hit nowhere near his intended target, instead striking a large boulder in front of him. There was a sharp crack that echoed through the silence.

"What was that?" Tanner asked, sniffing the air again.

"It's the bear!" Maurice said, spotting Teddy's fluffy head as he glanced out over the stones.

Tanner snarled at Maurice. "I told you to take care of him before we left with the others. Come on! Let's finish this once and for all!"

Maurice and Tanner left the fire and sprinted toward their den. Teddy jumped over the wall and tried to load another rock, but he was shaking so much, the stone slipped out of his hand. Tanner bolted up the incline and crept closer to the bear, growling as he gnashed his sharp teeth at him.

"I guess we'll use you as a chew toy for some after dinner entertainment!"

As he hurried to retreat, Teddy tripped over the makeshift stone wall, landing on his back. His heart raced as he scrambled to get up, and in doing so, pushed his feet forward, trying to crawl away. Along with the years of being pummeled by fallen trees, the wall had weakened. With Maurice and Tanner almost upon him, Teddy frantically kicked his feet. Several stones blocking the timbers broke loose, and the stones crumbled and rolled away. One of the larger boulders shifted and broke free, tumbling toward Tanner. The wolf's eye grew wide as he retreated down the embankment. Teddy jumped over a log that was behind him, but the only thing keeping that in place was the same freed boulder now rolling into the woods. Now, unencumbered, the timber shifted and rolled as well!

Tanner and Maurice were already making their way back up the incline toward Teddy when the log came bounding down on them.

"Watch out!" Tanner yelled to Maurice as the two jumped back.

The log bounced down on top of the den, collapsing the wolves' home. Once it was done with that, it hit the ground with a deep rumble and started rolling faster and faster toward the pair. Maurice and Tanner took off running after the trunk crashed through the rotisserie, snuffing out the flames and sending Roxy flying into the air. The wolves' feet were brushing up against the wood as the log gained speed. Unfortunately for them, they were running out of ground and came to the edge of a deep ravine. There was no time to decide what to do. With a tree charging them from behind, and a fifty foot vertical drop in front of them, they had no other option. The pair jumped forward just before being crushed by the massive timber.

The last thing Teddy saw was the log rolling over the edge of the cliff and disappearing deep into the ravine with a thunderous crash.

CHAPTER THIRTEEN

THE RELUCTANT HERO

TEDDY SLOWLY STOOD AND put his paw to his mouth. "What did I do?" he asked, tiptoeing his way to the edge, but afraid to look over.

"Way to go, Teddy! Come get us out of here!" Thomas and Dorian were screaming from their entanglement.

The hero bear darted over to the net. Still holding on to the spear-shot, he used the sharpened blade to slice through the thick rope of Roxy's net. Once enough strands were cut, Thomas and Dorian slid through. Both of them grabbed Teddy and gave him an enormous hug before sprinting over to Roxy, who was still tied to the rotisserie, motionless. Wisps of smoke drifted up from her fur, so Thomas patted her to snuff out any flames.

"Roxy! Hey, Roxy, are you still with us?" he asked as he took the spear and cut her loose from the steel spit.

Roxy's limp body rolled over, her arms falling to either side of her. Thomas and Dorian both shook her as a dejected Teddy slowly walked up to them and glanced over Thomas' shoulder.

"Roxy, please wake up," Thomas cried. "Come on, Roxy."

When nothing happened, he stopped shaking her and sat back on his heels.

"We're too late," he said, dropping his head.

The three of them looked to the ground before getting up. Thomas took Roxy's spear-shot and placed it in her hand and across her chest.

"You're a true warrior," he said before the trio turned and walked away.

Thomas picked up Teddy and hugged him again. "Thank you! You saved us."

"I could've done more. If I had been braver, quicker, then maybe —"

"Don't talk like that. You did great."

Thomas held Teddy tight and carried him away as the bear looked back at his friend. Out of nowhere, Roxy's body jerked and her paw shot to her mouth as she started hacking.

"Roxy!" Teddy wriggled his way free from Thomas and darted over to her. "You're alive!"

"I am," she said through half-opened eyes, still coughing the smoke out of her lungs. "What happened? How?"

Thomas dropped to his knees and hugged the raccoon. "It was all Teddy's doing. He saved all of us!"

"Really?" she said with a huge smile on her face. "I don't know what to say." She reached over and rubbed the top of his fluffy head. "I never would've guessed you were a bear of such strength and magnitude."

"Uhm, thank you, I think?"

"No, truly, thank you, Theodore. Hey, what happened to those two idiots?"

"I only saw them until just before they disappeared over the embankment," Thomas said. "We're not really sure what happened after that."

"Do you think they're still down there, waiting to attack us?" Dorian asked, chewing on his nails.

Thomas helped Roxy to her feet. After she peeled off the rope, she threw it to the ground and ran over to the edge of the ravine. She inched her way closer and peered over.

"That's a heck of a drop," Dorian said.

Deep below, at the bottom of the gorge, they saw Tanner's and Maurice's legs sticking out from under the huge log.

"Serves 'em right!" she said, a tear escaping from her eye. She stared up at the sky. "I'm sorry I couldn't have done this sooner, dad. You might have still been with us."

Thomas patted her on the back and then rubbed Teddy's head.

"So exactly what happened to you guys after we went to bed?"

"I'm not sure how they did it, but those two bungling idiots snuck up on us. I thought I was better than that."

"Yeah, they got the jump on all of us," Thomas said. "I heard some commotion, and when I woke up, Tanner was right over me, staring into my eyes. All I saw were his humongous fangs! I looked over and saw Maurice had his mouth wrapped tight around Roxy's throat. Dorian was half-asleep and stumbling about, trying to figure out what to do next. I don't know if they didn't notice you, or didn't think you were a threat, so they just left you alone."

"It's a good thing they did. Who knows what would've happened if you didn't save us?" Roxy said. "How did you track us?"

"I saw some footprints on the ground and followed them as far as I could. Then I got to the edge of this nightmarish place and had no idea where to go. Whoever thought of leaving that snack wrapper behind saved the day. I don't think I would've ever found any of you, or knew where this place was."

99

"Uhm, sorry about eating the last bag, Teddy. I got hungry as they marched us over here."

Teddy's mouth dropped as he stared at Dorian. *Was that really the last bag?* he thought as he counted them out in his head. Deep inside, his blood boiled, but if it hadn't been for Dorian's insatiable appetite, he may have gotten here too late.

"That's fine," Teddy said through gritted teeth. "Now, how 'bout we get out of here? This place gives me the creeps."

"Good idea," Roxy said, looking back toward the demolished rotisserie.

"Are you sure you're okay?" Thomas asked.

"Yeah," Roxy said, brushing her arms. "My fur is a little singed, but it's a lot better than the alternative. So, what are you going to do now? We can't go back to the mill. The Screech knows we were there and may go back to find us. Maybe you should just go home to your mom."

Thomas shook his head. "I can't. What will happen to Teddy?"

"Your mom can't be so mad at you that she would get rid of your best friend. Did you try talking to her before you left?"

"No."

Roxy grabbed his hand. "I lost my family. Don't lose yours."

"If we just find her, she'll fix everything. She promised."

"Who?"

"The Golden Pixie."

Roxy shook her head. "Well, we don't know where the Golden Pixie is. What are you going to do, wander the woods until she magically appears? And even if we do somehow find her, and she helps us get rid of The Screech, what then? Are you going to live in the woods for the rest of your life, scrounging for food, running away from more Tanners, or whatever other threats are out there?"

"You guys do it, why can't I?"

"Because your mom isn't here. Who's home taking care of her right now? You're not the only one who lost someone. She lost her husband, her best friend, and now you. Can you imagine how she feels? You need to be there to hold her hand. To help her get through all the same feelings you're having, too. She needs you, Thomas. And that crazy bear of yours."

Thomas stopped and sat on the ground. Nothing had worked out since he left home. He was constantly in fear of being captured by The Screech. He had almost been dinner for two maniacal wolves, and he was cold and hungry. Back when he was with his mom, he was none of these.

"Maybe you're right." He turned to Teddy. "It's time for us to go home."

Chapter Fourteen
OUR LAST MEAL

ROXY SMILED AND PUT her hand on Thomas' shoulder. "You won't regret it. Now, we just need to come up with a plan. Where exactly are we, anyway? I've never been this deep into the forest before."

Thomas pulled out his map and pointed to a corner section of the paper that was labeled 'The Darkness!'. "I think we're somewhere in this area."

"What is that?" Dorian asked.

"I'm not sure, but my parents would never go here when we went hiking. They told me it was haunted by the spirits of the warriors who once roamed this land."

Dorian scrunched his head down into his shoulders, his eyes darting around. "They might be on to something."

"Well, Tanner and Maurice were comfortable living here, so there must be something wrong with the place," Teddy said, creeping closer to Thomas.

Roxy shook her head and pushed past them. "Sounds like a bunch of mumbo jumbo. The sun is over that way and it's past noon, so that must be west. We need to go east to get to Toad Hollow, which will get you closer to home, so let's head this way." She pointed her spear-shot to a part of the forest that was even darker than the woods they were standing in. The branches from the trees seemed to reach forward. It appeared as though the tree limbs were either pushing explorers away from this place, or they were ready to grab anyone foolish enough to travel this way.

"Isn't there a bright field with pretty flowers we can hike through?" Teddy asked.

"Nope. That's the way!" Roxy insisted, as she headed out.

The rest of the group stared at each other. Thomas shook his head, drawing in a deep breath before he set off after Roxy. Dorian climbed on Thomas' back.

"Wait a minute. Why can't I get a ride?" Teddy asked, staring at Dorian, who was now slumped over the backpack, already asleep.

"Because if we let him walk, we'll never get there. Do you want to spend extra time in this part of the woods?"

Teddy looked at Thomas, then at the surrounding trees. It looked like something straight out of a horror film. The canopy was so thick, only scant flashes of sunlight were able to break past. Even the shadows haunted them as the darkness shifted with each step and leapt out from the trees. All the undergrowth was dead and shriveled up. Even the forest creatures had fled this portion of land.

"No, you're right. We should just keep moving."

There were no trails in this section of woods, and the group crunched through the remains of the dense carpet, struggling to keep track of where the sun was.

Roxy had her hands on her hips, staring up at the trees.

"I'm not even sure we'll be able to tell when it's nightfall. I've never seen it so dark during the day."

But Teddy had moved on from his fear and was now rubbing his stomach, which grumbled with each step.

"I'm starving. When can we eat?"

Thomas looked around. He, too, was hungry and could use a break. "Yeah, we should stop."

"I'll scout up ahead to make sure we're not being walking into an ambush," Roxy said, tightening her bandoliers across her chest before scampering off into the shadows.

After shaking Dorian awake, the group sat next to one of the ancient timbers that was the least intimidating. It looked less like a monster with razor-sharp claws and more like an old tree that had given up on life and was waiting to rot away. All of its leaves had dropped, large chunks of bark were missing, and branches were slowly breaking off.

"Okay, let's pool our resources," Thomas said, dumping out his backpack. Several bags of Cheesy Poofs fell out, along with two bottles of water, four granola bars, and an apple. "What do you guys have?"

Teddy and Dorian looked at each other, then at Thomas.

"I don't have any pockets?" Teddy said, shrugging his shoulders.

"I've got a few burs," Dorian said, plucking the prickly hitchhikers off his fur.

Thomas raised his eyes and shook his head. "Well, I guess we'll see what Roxy has when she gets back."

With a loud thud, Roxy dropped to the ground from above, causing the trio to jump.

"Did you realize you can leap from tree branch to tree branch and never have to touch the ground here? It's amazing!" she said with a broad smile on her face.

"You nearly scared us to death!"

"Oh, don't be ridiculous! So, there's nobody around for as far as I can see. What have you guys been up to?"

"We were just sitting down to eat, but wanted to wait for you. This is all we have. Do you have anything extra?"

"Let me check."

Roxy lifted the flap on her hip bag and shuffled her hand inside. She pulled out two apples, a handful of walnuts, and a small jar of honey.

"That's about it," she said, looking up with her tongue poking out of the corner of her mouth, her hand fishing through the bag. "Yup, that's all."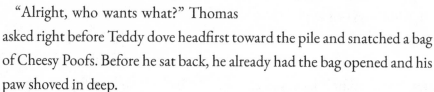

She plopped down next to the others and added her bounty to the pile.

"Alright, who wants what?" Thomas asked right before Teddy dove headfirst toward the pile and snatched a bag of Cheesy Poofs. Before he sat back, he already had the bag opened and his paw shoved in deep.

"What?" he asked. "I thought we were ready to eat?"

The others shook their heads and divvied up the remaining lot. "We'll have to share the water," Thomas said. "Roxy, would you mind splitting one with Dorian, and I'll share mine with Teddy?"

"Sounds good." She picked up the burs and handed them to Dorian. "Here. You can have these back."

Dorian smiled and hastily reattached them to his fur.

After eating, Thomas packed up the remaining food, which wasn't much. Roxy made sure they were heading east before they set off. The forest was quiet as the companions weaved their way through the thick bushes. Only their footsteps broke the unsettling silence. After several hours of hiking through thickets, mud, and over rotting timbers, Roxy stopped and glanced up to the sky.

"I'd hate to say this, but it's getting late. I think it's best if we set up some shelter for the night and start fresh in the morning."

Teddy and Dorian looked at each other. Both of their jaws dropped. "Here? You can't be serious!" Teddy said. "Nothing good can come from this."

"I don't think we have much choice. Believe it or not, it's going to get darker. Sorry. Now, I'm gonna clear out a spot and build a fire. Why don't y'all gather up enough wood to make it through the night?"

"Come on guys," Thomas said, grabbing Dorian and Teddy by their arms.

"But, but there —"

"It'll be fine, you crazy bear."

Dorian's eyes couldn't possibly open any wider as the three of them softly stepped into the shadows.

"Look around for some dry pieces. No rotted ones either," Thomas said, somehow feeling the need to whisper.

As they scavenged the ground, each crack of a branch, or crunch of leaves, made their heads pop up and scan the woods. Teddy was so low, it looked as though he was crawling along on his belly during his scavenging; Dorian was haphazardly grabbing blindly at the ground, keeping his focus up and ahead of him the whole time.

"You guys are being ridiculous," Thomas said, right before he heard a faint creaking in the distance.

CHAPTER FIFTEEN

STRANGE SOUNDS IN THE NIGHT

"**D**ID YOU GUYS HEAR that?" Thomas asked. "Guys?"

But Teddy and Dorian couldn't hear him because they were already sprinting back toward the campsite. At least Teddy was sprinting. His little blue feet were kicking up debris as he scrambled away. Thomas wasn't sure what Dorian was doing. It looked like someone trying to run while they were waist deep in syrup. Thomas reached down and gathered the wood they dropped before they abandoned him. With his arms full of stacked wood, and the pile reaching up to his nose, he set off after them.

By the time he got back to camp, Teddy was already spinning a horrific tale about a snaggle-toothed monster lurking through the shadows. He stood before Roxy with his arms spread wide.

"It was ten times larger than The Screech."

"Hey, thanks for helping, Ted!"

Ted? Oh, boy... he's angry.

"Thomas! Hey! Wow, that was scary. Anyway, I rushed back here to make sure I warned Roxy so she could prepare our defenses."

Thomas didn't say anything. He dropped his armful of wood onto a pile next to the spot Roxy had cleared and stood silent. Dorian dashed, or in his case, laggardly strolled into the campsite, out of breath. "I made it!" he said, crumpling to the ground, gasping for air.

"What happened?" Roxy asked, staring at the pathetic pile of logs.

"I, or obviously, 'we' heard a metal creaking off in the distance. Right after that, my so-called helpers bailed on me," he said, leering at the bear and sloth who refused to make eye contact with him.

"Could you see what it was?" Roxy asked.

"No. It was too far off. You don't think it could be The Screech, do you?"

"I don't reckon so. You said it's never traveled off the paths or roads. Regardless, I should go check it out just in case."

"I can come help," Thomas said, standing.

"No, you stay here. I can move quickest through the trees. Besides, someone has to protect these two," she said, looking over at Teddy and Dorian, who were huddled together, their heads on pivots as they scanned the trees. "Wait until I return to build the fire. If it is The Screech, you don't want to draw it to us."

It seemed like hours had passed since Roxy left. "I hope she's okay," Thomas said, right before some rustling in the trees made them jump. Roxy fell to the ground and rolled before standing up.

"Hey, guys."

"Geez. Did you really have to do that?" Teddy asked, his paw on his chest as he gasped.

Roxy tried to hold it in, but then burst out laughing. "Mr. Bear, you are priceless," she said, shaking her head as she walked over to the pile of logs. With her knife and piece of flint, she set them ablaze and warmed her hands.

"Did you find anything?" Thomas asked.

"Yeah. It was just an old pickup truck. Some bootlegger must've left that scrap heap here from back when there were moonshiner stills all over these woods. The thing is all sorts of rusted. Some squirrels must've jumped on it and made all that ruckus. You know how those pesky critters like to goof around."

With the fire roaring, the group sat around the warmth of the flames and finished the remaining food.

"That's the last of it," Thomas said, shaking his backpack.

Teddy's orange stained jaw dropped. "What are we gonna do for food now?"

"Well, until we make it home, we'll eat what we find. Roxy can help us out with that."

"Sure can. There's enough food growing in this forest to feed us for the rest of our lives. There are mushrooms, roots, berries, nuts —"

She stopped when she noticed Teddy staring at her with dull eyes.

"I meant REAL food," he said, shaking his empty Cheesy Poofs bag.

"It'll be fine," Thomas said. "You can survive for a few days without them."

Teddy crumpled to the ground and crossed his arms.

"Has he always been like this?" Roxy asked.

Thomas smiled and sat next to her in front of the fire. "Yeah. He is set in his ways, that's for sure."

"What's wrong with knowing what you like and what you want out of life?" Teddy asked. "Take Dorian, for instance."

The lethargic sloth lay sprawled out on a large log near the fire, passed out. He was using a large rock as a pillow, contorting his neck to a 90-degree angle.

"How does he do that?" Thomas asked. "It's like he doesn't have any bones."

"He enjoys sleeping, but nobody gives him a hard time."

"We're not trying to give you a hard time. You are very particular and always have been. I remember back when I first started getting an allowance. My parents took me shopping. Teddy was with us, of course, because we're never separated. In the store was a nice shirt and tie that would've fit you perfect. But you wouldn't even try it on."

"I'm not replacing my red bowtie. It suits me quite well."

"But you might have liked this other tie. You hate change and were too stubborn to even try it on."

Teddy stood and glared at Thomas. "Well, I am going to sleep. Thanks for the food, ROXY." He turned and walked over to the lean-to Roxy built and curled up in a ball.

"Are you guys gonna be okay?" she asked.

"Yeah. We bicker every now and then, but that's just the way it is. We always make up later."

"Hmm."

"What?" Thomas asked.

"Oh, sorry. I was thinking that would've been a better approach to take with your mother. If nothing else, it might've helped you avoid all this Screech nonsense."

Thomas creaked out a smile and nodded. "I guess you're right. It's just that I see Teddy as more of a friend. She's a mom. I don't think her and I connected as well as me and Teddy. Teddy and I talk about everything. What I did in school, what I want to be when I get older, even how I felt about my father dying."

"Well, aren't you like a parent to that crazy bear of yours? What if he did the same to you?"

112

"What do you mean?"

"Look, I'm not saying you're wrong or anything like that, but what if Teddy ignored you or dismissed anything you had to say? I don't think you two would be nearly as close. Anyway, it's not my place to say, but could it be you never gave your mom the same chance? Do you tell her about your day, your hopes and dreams? Or do you come home, grumble a few words and brush her off? That's what I used to do with my dad. It kills me every time I think back to it. All of that time I wasted when I could've been talking to him. But that's just me."

"No, no, it's not," Thomas said, staring off into the darkness.

They sat quietly and listened to the crackle of the fire.

"Has it been hard? Do you miss him?" Thomas asked.

Roxy nodded her head. "Every day. Just as I'm sure you miss your dad. We used to hang out all the time. Then, when I got a little older, I thought I knew everything. I barely talked to him and went off on my own more than I did before. But he always understood. Gave me my space. It wasn't until it was too late before I realized what I was missing. Now, I can't get any of it back. When we get you home, don't make the same mistakes I did. Make sure you cherish the time you have with your family because you'll never get it back."

Thomas sat silent for a while before nodding his head. "I'm sorry about your dad, Roxy. Maybe, when this is all done, you can be part of our family."

Roxy looked up and creaked out a smile. "I'd like that."

A loud snort from a curled up bear interrupted their moment, as Teddy rolled over, sound asleep and snoring. Roxy and Thomas laughed as they looked at him with his mouth drooping open.

"He's a great friend," Thomas said.

"You're lucky to have him. Well, I guess we should call it a night and get an early start. I'll pile some more wood on the fire to get us through until morning. Should we wake Dorian?"

Thomas looked over and noticed the sloth had contorted himself to where his head rested on the ground, with one leg over the fallen log, and the other resting high against a branch. "No. Oddly enough, he looks comfortable. I say just let him sleep."

Chapter Sixteen

REFLECTIONS OF HOME

B Y THE TIME THOMAS woke up, the fire had long since burnt out and smoke lazily rose from the heap of ashes in the pit. He shivered as he rubbed his hands together and placed them near the remaining embers that flickered with a faint orange glow. Roxy was already awake and gathering up her gear.

"Good morning, Roxy."

"Hey. I'm gonna run out and gather up some food before those two knuckleheads wake up. You know how irritable they can be when they're hungry."

"Do you need help?"

"Nah, just make sure the fire is completely out if you can. Freakishly scary woods or not, I'd hate to have an accident and burn this place down."

Thomas chuckled as Roxy made her way deeper into the woods. He walked over to the firepit and kicked dirt onto the remaining logs to snuff out any embers still burning. Once he was certain he got them all, he sat down and retrieved his map before fishing a pencil out of his backpack. After getting his bearings, he sketched in a new location on the paper, along with a sketch of the old rusted truck that Roxy found. For the caption, he labeled this spot "The Friendship Circle."

"What are you doing?" Teddy asked, walking over and smacking his lips.

"Just updating the map. Are you still angry, or are we good now?"

"Nah, we're good," he said, slapping Thomas on the shoulder and dropping down next to him. "I think I was just tired and hungry." Dorian was still in the same position he was in before they went to bed. "Where's Roxy?"

"She said she was going to scrounge up some breakfast."

Dorian's head shot up. "Breakfast?"

Thomas smiled. "Good morning, Dorian. Yeah. Roxy left to find us some food." The disheveled sloth unfolded himself from his awkward sleeping position. "Doesn't your neck hurt now?"

"Huh? Nah, not at all." Dorian twisted his neck, which caused several loud cracks that were so unsettling, you'd think he'd just suffered a horrible death. Both Teddy and Thomas cringed at the noise. "Geez, Dorian. It sounded like someone crushed a handful of walnuts."

"Mmm! I could go for some walnuts right now."

"How much longer until we get home?" Teddy asked.

"I'm not sure." Thomas placed his pencil on the sheet of paper and measured the distance. "We have a whole pencil length to go before we even get back to Roland's boat. At least it's that far away if I calculated this right."

"What are you guys going to do when you get home?"

"Well, I plan on taking a nice hot eucalyptus bath and shampooing my fur. I mean, look at it! I'm an absolute wreck," Teddy said, plucking bits of dried mud from his stomach. "My shipment of jasmine shampoo should arrive before we get home."

"What about you, Thomas?"

Thomas looked at the pair and smiled. "I'm going to hug my mom and never let go."

Out of nowhere, the sound of twigs snapping filled the air as something came charging through the bushes in the distance. It was Roxy! She scrambled out of the brush and blew right past them.

"Run!"

Chapter Seventeen

HE'S GONE

"WHAT HAPPENED?" THOMAS ASKED as they scrambled out of the campsite, trying to keep up with Roxy.

"The Screech! It's coming this way! I don't know how, but it found us."

"We were careful! We're not on any trails!"

"Apparently it doesn't care. Let's go!"

The group heard squeaking and clanking in the distance.

Dorian was already falling behind. "I'm just gonna slow you guys down," Dorian said, as he stopped running and scampered up a nearby tree. "Don't worry, it'll never see me."

They all looked at each other, and then up to the sloth. "Okay, but once you get up there, hide and don't move until we come get you."

Dorian climbed high in the tree and blended into the thickest patch of leaves he could find. The awful sound of rattling metal grew louder and louder as The Screech crashed through the overgrown underbrush.

"That blasted thing is too fast! We have to split up!" Roxy said. "I'll try to draw it out my way. When it gets close, I'll scurry up into the trees as well. Go that way," she said, pointing to a nearby clearing. "There's a path up ahead. You guys can get away quicker on that!"

Thomas clutched Teddy's paw. "Roxy, please be careful."

"You too. When we lose that thing, I'll grab Dorian and come find you!"

Roxy snatched a nearby stick, using to it smack the trees as she zigzagged her way through the bushes, trying to make as much noise as she could.

Thomas and Teddy took off running, and after breaking through the brush, they reached the path.

"How far do we go?" Teddy asked, huffing and puffing.

"Roxy said to keep going. Don't worry, she'll find us."

They ran as far for as long as they could before stopping to catch their breath. Once they did, they sprinted a little farther, but abruptly stopped because the trail broke off into two separate paths leading away from each other.

"Which way now?" Teddy asked, but there wasn't enough time to decide, for not too far behind them The Screech had ignored Roxy and was barreling its way toward them, clouds of smoke drifting away in its wake.

"It followed us instead!" Thomas said, staring at Teddy. The pair glanced at their surroundings.

Thomas was visibly shaking. He dropped to the ground and covered his head with his arms.

"I don't know what else to do."

Teddy drew in a deep breath and placed his paw on Thomas' shoulder.

"We have to split up," the tiny bear said. "It's the only way."

Thomas' head shot up.

"What? No! I don't want to leave you!" He reached forward and grabbed Teddy's arms. "You're everything to me." The tears in his eyes were clouding his vision.

"It's our best chance. And don't worry about me. I'm very nimble."

After wiping his eyes, Thomas brought Teddy close and hugged him tight, sobbing. "I can't imagine a world without you! I don't want to be alone."

"You're not alone," Teddy said, rubbing his head. "I am always with you, whether you see me or not."

"Wait!"

"What? We are running out of time."

Thomas looked at the ground. "I'm scared."

Teddy let out a deep breath. "Of course you're scared. You'd be crazy not to be. But fear won't protect you. It will control you if you give it the chance. Use it to make yourself stronger. Turn it into anger."

He pushed Thomas away and looked around.

"Now go, before The Screech catches us both. And whatever you do, don't ever quit!"

Thomas stared at him, unable to stop shaking.

"Go!" Teddy yelled.

Thomas stood and turned toward the other path. Gripping his fists tight, he stomped his foot on the ground, his face contorted with sadness as he ran down the path. Teddy watched until he disappeared around a bend.

"Goodbye, my friend."

With the ominous shadow about to overtake him, Teddy slowly trotted down his path, waving his arms in the air, making certain The Screech knew to follow him. Thomas leapt over some rotted logs and hid behind them, still able to spot Teddy as he ran.

Faster! Please, you have to run faster!

Thomas hoped Teddy could sense his pleas for the little bear with the tiny legs to run faster, but then he heard that terrible sound. The howling of a determined monster in pursuit of its prey. As soon as the noise appeared, so did the foreboding shadow as it spilled across the path and

121

overtook Teddy. And just as quick as it appeared, the shadow passed and Teddy was gone.

CHAPTER EIGHTEEN
THE SUSPECT

"T HIS IS THE THIRD time we've been through here. Can't we go get lunch?"

Spiller stared blankly at Bushner. "No! The report said there's been a suspicious gray van lurking around here. Traffic cameras also picked up the same van in the area during the exact time someone saw Thomas entering the woods. I don't think that was a coincidence."

"We get calls like this all the time. Did they say why the van was suspicious?"

"Only that it had been through here all day. The complainant said the driver was acting as though he was searching for something; driving slowly and looking all around. Plus, none of the neighbors have seen that van before."

There was a loud squeal of worn out brakes just ahead.

"Hey! Is that it?"

An older gray van with large patches of rust turned the corner. A piece of frayed rope was the only thing holding the hood down, and the engine was clearly visible through gaping holes in the fenders and grill. Chunks of mud flew off the worn tires as it turned down the street. Spillen tried to read the numbers on the license plate, but it flopped around as it dangled off the back bumper, held on by one zip tie.

"That's the van," Spillen said, picking up the police radio. "1525 dispatch, we have the van in sight. We'll be conducting a traffic stop at Colson Avenue and 23rd."

"Colson and 23rd, copy."

Spillen turned the emergency lights on, but the van didn't stop. It swerved slightly before straightening out again.

"What's he doing?" Bushner asked.

"I don't know. Maybe he's drunk."

Spillen hit the siren, and the driver pulled over to the side of the road. The two detectives got out and cautiously approached the van on opposite sides. They tried to look in the rear windows, but the dark tint covering them made it impossible to see through. Once Spillen got to the driver's side window, she tapped on the glass, her hand close to her gun. The driver looked as rough as his van. He was an older man with thinning, scraggly salt and pepper hair and a thick scruffy face. With his soiled hands, he reached down and lowered the window. An odor of stale cigarette smoke and gasoline spilled out from the inside.

"What now?" the surly man asked as he sat unmoving in a stained, off-white t-shirt, both of his hands holding firm on to the steering wheel.

"Good afternoon, sir. I'm Detective Laura Spillen. We're looking for a small boy. Have you seen him?" she asked as she held out a photo of Thomas.

"No," the man grumbled without even looking at the picture.

Spillen glanced over to Bushner, who was watching from the passenger's side.

"Why is there a smell of gasoline?"

The man closed his eyes and raised his eyebrows. "Because my gas gauge is broke so I carry extra with me just in case I run out."

"Okay, well, we've received phone calls from the residents in this neighborhood that a suspicious van was driving up and down the roads and into the woods. They were concerned because they've never seen your van here before."

"Well, it's a public road and a public forest, so they can mind their own business. I have every right to be here."

"Do you have any identification on you? A driver's license?" she asked.

"What for? I've done nothing wrong."

"Well, your vehicle is in pretty rough shape," Spillen said, looking up and down the battered van. "Let's see, broken exhaust, cracked windshield — does this thing even have brakes? It sounded like metal on metal when you stopped. How did you pass the inspection? Oh wait, that's expired as well," she said, glancing at the inspection sticker.

"What's in the van?" Bushner asked, shining his light into the back of the van.

"None of your business, that's what." The driver adjusted his glasses and fumbled through his wallet. "Here's my driver's license. Is there anything else, or can you two find something better to do with your time?"

"Hey, Spillen," Bushner called out.

She took the man's license and walked over to the passenger side of the van where Bushner was standing. He nodded to the inside of the van. Spillen glanced in the window and on the floorboard was a tiny, fuzzy blue leg wedged under the seat. The two detectives looked at each other and then walked back over to the driver's side.

"We'll be right back."

Spillen's mind raced as she tried to come up with ways to detain this person. After calling in his driver's license number, she turned to Bushner. "He's awful nervous. Do you think he'll talk?"

Bushner looked over. "No. But I think we should bring him in and question him, anyway. Maybe we'll get lucky."

Spillen nodded. "That'll give us time to get a warrant for the van." Both detectives stepped up to the door. "Mr. Krantz, I need you to step out of the vehicle."

"Why?"

"You need to step out now, and keep your hands where I can see them."

Krantz fidgeted with his fingers on the steering wheel as his eyes darted back and forth.

"I'm not going to tell you again," Detective Spillen said, watching as the man's forehead beaded up with sweat.

In the distance, sirens wailed as the backup police cars approached. Krantz glanced up at his rearview mirror.

"Don't do anything stupid," Detective Bushner warned him.

With that, the man squeezed the steering wheel before reaching his hand out and pulling on the door handle. As the van door squeaked opened, he slowly stepped out. The detectives grabbed him by the arms and spun him around before placing him in handcuffs.

Spillen opened the passenger's side door and reached below the seat with a pen, using it to slide out a soiled, light blue stuffed bear. In the back of the van was a red plastic gas can, shovels, rope, and duct tape.

"Where's the kid?" Bushner asked.

"Don't know what you're talking about." The driver smugly smiled.

Spillen threw the man up against the side of his van. "Then where did that bear come from?"

"It's my grandkid's toy. Is that a crime now?"

"It's exactly like the one the missing boy had with him," she said, pushing the picture of Thomas into the man's face.

Krantz glared at her. "And you don't think the toy company made more than one? Now I know why you're just a cop."

As soon as the other cars arrived, Spillen dragged Krantz to the backseat of one and pushed him in, slamming the door shut.

Bushner got into Krantz's van to move it closer to the curb and out from the middle of the road until the tow truck came. "Hey, Spillen, you need to move the cruiser back. This thing won't shift into drive, so I'll have to back it up."

"Okay. Hey, Ben. Can you watch him for me?" she asked an officer standing next to her just as her radio chirped.

"I don't know how this thing is still running," Bushner said. "The transmission sticks and all you can do is put it in reverse to free it up. How does he drive this piece of junk?"

"Yeah. This guy has duct tape holding the red lenses on his taillights. It makes them look like eyes scowling," the officer told her.

Spillen got into her car and backed up, giving Bushner more room. After talking to the dispatcher, she walked up to him.

"Dispatch called back. They confirmed he's on the offender's list."

Bushner shook his head, glaring at Krantz. "Are we close enough to the school to make a charge stick?"

Spillen looked around. "I'm not sure, but with everything else, it's at least enough to bring him in and talk to him." She walked up to the officer standing watch over Krantz. "Hey, Ben. If his van doesn't fall apart, we're going to have that thing towed. Bushner and I are going to stay here and write out the tow sheet. Can you do me a favor and bring Krantz to the station? Just stick him in an interview room until we can get there."

"Yeah, no problem. If you need anything else, just call me."

CHAPTER NINETEEN
WE NEED A PLAN

"TEDDY?"

But it was useless. The Screech had long since vanished. Even its celebratory smoke was gone, as was his friend. Thomas stood frozen, his mouth wide open, refusing to believe what had just happened.

"No..."

Thomas ran down the trail, but The Screech was nowhere in sight.

"Teddy!" He kept running, calling out to his bear until he was too exhausted to go any further.

His eyes filled with tears and his lower lip quivered as he stared at the empty path in front of him. Unable to control his sobs, his legs gave out, and he crumpled to the ground, dropping his head to his hands. His dearest friend in the world had been consumed by The Screech and he was gone forever.

Roxy and Dorian found him sitting alone, cross-legged in the dirt, weeping into his arms.

"What's wrong? Where's Teddy?" she asked, looking around.

Thomas stared up at them, his eyes red and swollen as tears streamed down his face. "The — the — it was The Screech. It got to him."

He barely managed to get the words out before his emotions swept over him and his head dropped back into his arms.

"He sacrificed himself to save me."

"No," Dorian said, falling to his knees and throwing his arm over Thomas.

Roxy stabbed her spear-shot to the ground and stomped her feet, screaming to the sky. "That's it!" She turned to Thomas, gritting her teeth. "We need to get rid of that obnoxious beast once and for all! Which direction did it go? We have to mount a rescue operation and get our bear back!"

Thomas heaved out a sigh and pointed down the path. Roxy stared ahead at the empty path and paced. "We need a plan. Thomas! Get over here. Help me think of one."

Thomas dragged himself up and walked over to her, sniffling. She grabbed him by the shirt and looked into his eyes. "There's no time for that now," she told him. "We have a bear to save! Where's your map?"

He pulled the tattered paper from his pocket and spread it out before them. Roxy dropped to the ground and studied the drawing.

"What is 'Turnaround Swamp?'"

Thomas creaked out a smile. "That's the swamp by Roland's house. Anytime we got close to it, my dad would say, 'Well, I guess it's time to turnaround.' Teddy hated going there."

Roxy smiled. "You still got your pencil?"

Thomas reached into his bag and retrieved it for her.

"Okay," she said, drawing the two trails they were on and looking up at the sky. "East is this way, but The Screech went west. It must've thought you dropped Teddy and kept going, hoping to catch up to you."

Roxy jumped up and tapped the pencil against her lip.

"When it can't find you, my guess is it will circle around and come this way. This is great!"

"What do you mean?"

"You'll see. I have the perfect plan. I just need to work out the details. We're gonna get that crazy bear back!"

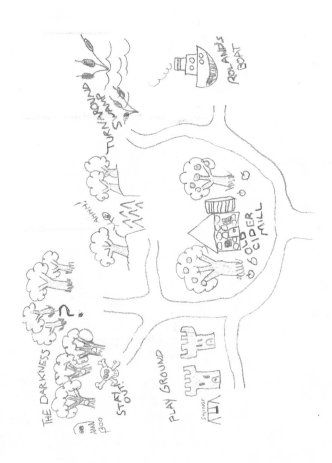

CHAPTER TWENTY

RELEASED

"**H**EY, YOU'RE NOT GOING to like this."

Spillen dropped her face into her hands. "You mean aside from Krantz lawyering up and walking out of here with that big stupid, smug smile on his face? What now?"

"Yeah, uhm, he went to the tow yard and got his van back."

"Are you kidding me?" she blurted out, slamming her fists onto her desk. "How?"

"Since Krantz wasn't close enough to the school to bring charges, the judge wouldn't grant us authority to place a hold on the van or give us a search warrant. She also said there wasn't enough probable cause for anything else, his phone records, his apartment, nothing. She even chastised me, warning me we were getting close to harassment against him. Can you believe that? A kid's missing and she is more concerned about Krantz's feelings! Anyway, the owner of the tow company couldn't do anything about it. He had to give Krantz the van back."

Spillen ran her fingers through her hair. "Krantz is dirty. I know he is."

She stood and walked over to a cork board hanging on the wall. On it, she had pinned Thomas' picture, a topographical map of Creekside Woods, and a photograph of the map Thomas had drawn that was hanging up in his room. Next to Thomas' picture, she pinned a copy of Krantz's driver's license and a picture of his van. She walked back over to her desk and sat down, reviewing the affidavit they had presented to the judge.

"I don't get it? What about the bear, the shovels, everything else we saw in his van?"

"The judge said the same thing Krantz did. Unless we have evidence that the bear Krantz has belonged to Thomas, she said she wouldn't authorize anything on it. I had to admit to her there wasn't anything written on the bear tying Thomas to it. No name, address, nothing. She laughed off everything else, saying it was an overreach. She even told me she has a shovel in her trunk for gardening at her mother's house. I'm kicking myself for not taking the bear when we had it and putting it on the tow inventory."

"That wouldn't have worked. Since we were just at Thomas' house, Krantz's attorney would claim cross-contamination for any hairs or fibers we found on the bear. This is ridiculous!" Spillen pushed her chair back so hard that it fell over. She grabbed her keys off the desk and stormed away.

"Where are you going?" Bushner asked.

"I'm going to find Krantz. Guys like him are cocky. And now he feels empowered. Either he knows where Thomas is or he's driving around looking for him. Either way, I'm going to catch him, and I know exactly where to look."

CHAPTER TWENTY-ONE

AN AMBUSH

R OXY YANKED HER SPEAR-SHOT out of the ground and dragged
the tip through the dirt as she sketched out a diagram. Meanwhile,
Thomas walked down the path and stared ahead to where The Screech
disappeared. Some bushes along the trail rustled, causing him to jump back
until he saw Roland step out of them, carrying a large wicker basket.

"Thomas! I was wondering who was making all that ruckus."

"Roland, what are you doing here?"

"Oh, my!" he said, rushing up to Thomas with a huge grin spread across
his face. "Don't tell anyone my secret, but the ground here is a perfect place
for truffles to grow." He opened the lid of his basket and showed Thomas
his treasure of rounded mushrooms that reminded Thomas of pieces of
coal. He glanced around before looking back at Thomas. "Hey, where's
that bear of yours?"

Thomas' eyes filled with tears. "The Screech took him."

"No!" Roland said, dropping his basket. "Where, when?"

"Just now. That noise you heard was The Screech."

Roland stared off into the distance. "I hate that thing! Do you have any
idea where they went?"

Thomas shook his head, unable to speak.

"Well, what can I do to help?"

A short distance away, Roxy was pacing, rubbing her chin with her hand. "This is gonna work!"

"Who's that?" Roland asked, blocking the sun from his eyes as he stared down the path.

"That's Roxy. She's been helping me search for the Golden Pixie. Dorian is down there too."

Roland and Thomas walked over to where Roxy and Dorian stood, looking down at her sketch.

"Roland! I haven't seen you in forever. How the heck are you?"

"I was doing good until Thomas told me what happened."

"Are you here to help?"

"I am now. I would do anything for my dear friend Thomas, and I suppose that bear of his too."

Roxy had a huge grin on her face. "This is perfect, guys. And Roland, you're a big part of this plan."

"Excellent!" Roland said, tapping his fingers together excitedly.

She used her spear to trace along while she explained the plan. "Okay, so we are here, and The Screech headed that way." She drew an arrow leading away from the group. "Since it only got to Teddy, it must still be close. My guess is that before too long, it will come back in this direction. That monster isn't going to give up so easily, so it must still be hunting for Thomas. I can't imagine it forgetting about him after it stole Teddy. Now, on our left is the swamp, and beyond that, Roland's house," she said, drawing a small boat in the middle of the wetland. "We need to lead The Screech to Roland's! Roland, do you still have all those barrels in the storage area of your boat?"

"Yes, I do. They used to haul their whiskey in them, but they're all empty."

"That's perfect! We need to gather up a couple of them, so if you can do that, it'd be a big help. In the meantime, we need to collect rocks and sticks so we can set up ammo dumps. We'll fill Roland's barrels with the rocks and sharpened sticks in these locations." She marked an 'X,' next to all the places near Roland's house where she wanted the barrels. "If we can do that, and lead The Screech to this area, it will get bogged down in the mud, then we'll have it trapped. Once that thing is stuck and can't escape, we can encircle it and destroy it once and for all!"

"Brilliant!" Dorian said.

"I agree," Roland said. "Once something as large as The Screech gets stuck in that slop, it's done for. Just like the dinosaurs in the tar pits."

Thomas thought for a moment. "But if we do this, you'll be putting yourself at risk! Plus, there's a chance everyone will find out about your house. They'll take it away from you."

"Maybe. But I can always move to another home. It is much harder to find a dear friend like you. Besides, I think I'm ready for a change. As a matter of fact, there's a little piece of land I've had my eye on for some time. It's closer to where the river is still running and there's an abandoned stone pump house. Reminds me of a castle, which I think is better suited for a toad of my stature. I mean, I am descended from knights."

Thomas creaked out a smile. "What do I get to do?"

"How attached are you to that backpack?" Roxy asked.

"It means nothing to me if I can get Teddy back."

"Good. Follow me."

They arrived at the split in the trail where they had encountered The Screech.

"What are we doing here?" Thomas asked.

"Well, if we lay your backpack on the ground here, right out in the open, The Screech will see it, or pick up your scent and know you're close by. When it's distracted by the bag, we'll jump out of the woods and startle it, forcing it to come this way. That is, if you feel strong enough to do that. Once The Screech sees you, we'll have it chase you into the swampy area here, near Roland's boat. You'll have the advantage because you know the rocks to jump across to get to Roland's. The Screech doesn't. It's bound to get bogged down in the muck, then we'll have it trapped and we can destroy it once and for all!"

Thomas' eyes darted back and forth and he was visibly shaking.

"I've seen The Screech run before. It's too fast. It'll catch me."

"You don't have to let it get that close. All it needs to do is catch sight of you. Roland, Dorian, and I will be nearby the whole time. When The Screech gets close enough, we'll attack it from all sides. It'll be so confused, it won't know what to do, or who to go after. There's no way that rascal will win!"

Thomas beamed as an enormous smile spread across his face. "That beast will never know what hit it! Let's do it!"

Thomas lay the bag on the ground right at the fork, which opened the trail to the right.

"Okay, let's go!" Roxy said.

"Wait!" Thomas reached in to the backpack and grabbed a picture from the inside pocket. It was his dad, wearing his military uniform. In his hand, he was holding Teddy. Thomas stared at the picture and smiled before sliding it into his back pocket. "Okay, I'm ready."

"Hey. What about me? I'm sure there's something I can do to help."

Roxy turned to Dorian. "You need to head to Roland's boat and find as many rocks as you can. Stack them in the barrels and on the deck of

Roland's boat, where they'll be easy to get to. We'll use them to throw at the beast."

Dorian slowly nodded his head and made his way through the brush.

"Roland, when you get done with the barrels, find some good solid sticks we can use as spears. Once you get to your house, sharpen the tips. That thing has a thick hide. I'm sure Dorian can help you with those barrels."

"Got it!" Roland said, as he grabbed his basket of truffles and sprinted away.

"Okay, Thomas. All you and I have to do now is wait here in the weeds until The Screech approaches. Once he does, we'll race out to Roland's house. Don't worry. There's no way that thing can catch us. It doesn't know the terrain like we do."

Roxanne and Thomas ducked under some bushes far ahead, but close enough to where they could still see the backpack.

"Thanks for staying with me," Thomas said.

"Are you kidding? This is awesome! I'm always ready to help the underdog. Don't worry, we're gonna get that thing once and for all!"

Thomas smiled and squeezed Roxanne's hand.

"I can't wait to get home and tell my mom."

"You miss her, don't you?"

"Yeah. I should've never left. It's just — it's just so tough now that my dad's gone. We were best friends. Now, seeing all these kids in school, their dads dropping them off, or coming to their games and events, I can't deal with it. I shouldn't have acted out like I did. My mom is always there to talk. She tries to every day. What was I thinking?"

"Hey, look. When I lost my dad, I was in a terrible place. My mom was gone long before that, so I was all alone. You had Teddy to lean on. I'm sure your mom regrets threatening to take him away from you. There's no doubt in my mind she would never have done that. My guess is she was frustrated. And alone. You two need each other."

Thomas nodded, still keeping a watchful eye out for The Screech.

"As soon as we defeat this monster, I'm going to make things right. My dad would want me to be there for my mom."

"Good for you, Thomas."

"Did your dad build your house?"

"No, it was my grandpappy. You think I'm tough? You should have met him. Nobody around could stand up to him. If he were still here, he'd be wearing Maurice and Tanner's hides as a coat. That fella could scare the stink back into a skunk."

Thomas laughed. "Well, he did a great job building that cabin. You're lucky to have such a nice home."

"Yeah, I am. But it can't compare to yours."

"What do you mean? You've never seen my house."

Roxy chuckled.

"You're thinking about this all wrong. The walls, pictures, furniture, none of that matters. You house has a mom. Nothing beats that."

Thomas thought about when he would wake up in the middle of the night and catch his mother covering him with a blanket; the countless times she picked Teddy up off the floor and tucked his bear in tight next to him; each morning she would wake Thomas up with a gentle rub on his head. She always greeted him after school with a hug, fixed his favorite meals, snuggled with him on the couch to watch their favorite shows. Not one of these memories showcased his home. Roxy was right. When he thought about all of this, all he saw was the moment, not the walls.

It wasn't long before there was a faint creaking in the distance. "Did you hear that?" Thomas asked.

Roxanne put her ear against the ground. "Something's definitely coming," she said.

Thomas' heart raced as the sound grew louder and louder.

"There it is!" Roxanne said, noticing some movement just ahead. Everything suddenly got quiet until in an instant The Screech burst through some thickets and belched out a squeal as it rushed forward.

Chapter Twenty-Two

THE GOLDEN PIXIE

THE RAGE OF THE menacing creature was obvious as it ripped through the soil, straining itself to catch up to its prey. As soon as the beast noticed the abandoned backpack, it came to a sudden stop. A chill ran up Thomas' spine as The Screech turned its massive body and bolted down the path, approaching the two friends hiding in the shadows. With an angered resolve, it let out another scream and charged toward the pair. Thomas' fear intensified as it spread through his body and caught in his throat. He struggled to move, to speak, until all at once he exploded with anguish. His words burst forth like steam escaping from a kettle.

"Let's go!"

Roxy stuck her hand up in the air.

"Not yet, Thomas. Just wait."

The Screech rumbled its way closer and closer to them. Thomas started fidgeting his hands, digging them into the dirt, preparing to dart out. His head pivoted from Roxy to the path as his heart thundered in his chest. About to explode from the nervous energy, he stood up, but Roxy grabbed his shirt and yanked him back down.

"Wait for it... wait for it," she said as The Screech drew closer. As soon as she smelled the noxious stench of the creature's breath, she let go of Thomas' shirt. "Okay now!" she yelled, pushing him away.

Thomas rocketed out of the bushes, startling The Screech, which skid along the dirt trail as it came to an abrupt stop. With a loud roar that reverberated through the forest and shook the leaves, it lunged toward Thomas, who was running as fast as he could, breaking through the dense weeds.

The Screech leapt from the trail and burst through the bushes, bouncing over the rough terrain as it rushed toward Thomas. With no regard for what was in its path, the hideous beast spit smoke and squealed excitedly as it approached its prey. Roxy had already crossed the swamp and made it to Roland's house by the time Thomas reached the edge of the swamp. He glanced back and saw the beast's crushing jaws as it was almost upon him. Thomas frantically looked ahead, trying to focus on his footwork as he jumped from one exposed stone to the next. Each time he landed on a rock, he turned his head, glancing back over his shoulder as The Screech came at him. Since the tide had come in, a thin layer of water now covered the mud. Not knowing its surroundings, The Screech lurched forward, causing a loud splash in the shallow water. The noise startled Thomas, which caused him to trip on a stone and fall into the muck. The weight of The Screech bogged down the creature as it floundered in the swampy soil. Angry roars erupted as it struggled to get its footing.

"Get up! It's right behind you!"

Thomas panicked, trying to scramble to his feet. The water grew dark from all the mud being churned up. Just behind him, he saw the eyes of the monstrous beast as it once again charged toward him, mud and weeds spewing out from its wake. It made a terrible grumbling noise as it struggled to make it through the slop and get to the boy. As Thomas regained his footing, he leapt from one rock to the next, hurrying as he saw Roland's boat just ahead. All he had to do was make it across several more stones and he would be safe. As he jumped over to the next one, his foot missed, and he slipped off the wet stone and into the thick mud. His leg sunk knee deep in the sludge and he was the one who was now trapped!

"I'm stuck!" he screamed.

The Screech never lost focus or gave up as it plowed its way toward him. The mud was up to the monster's eyes, but that didn't seem to slow it down. It kept churning along, creeping its was closer.

Roxy and Roland began their attack from the boat. Dorian was crouching in the weeds next to an overloaded barrel, doing the same. Their barrage filled the sky, as thick as a swarm of bees. The stones and sharpened sticks rained down and pummeled The Screech, but nothing penetrated its thick hide. It roared with each strike, refusing to give up now that it could taste Thomas' fear.

Thomas kept pulling on his leg, hoping to break free from the mud sucking him down. As he yanked, he unearthed a rock the size of a baseball. He grabbed hold of the stone and turned to The Screech. With all his might, he heaved the hefty stone right at The Screech's eyes, hoping to blind it. The rock struck its target and smoke billowed from The Screech's mouth.

Roland's eyes lit up. He ran inside his house and returned carrying his ancestor's medieval sword.

"Finish him off with this!" he said, tossing Thomas the weapon.

Thomas snatched the sword out of the air and held it high. Then, with all his strength, he hurled it forward as hard as he could. The world around Thomas seemed to slow down as the sword sliced through the air. With a deadly strike, the blade pierced the beast's armor and it let out a blood-curdling scream.

"You got him!"

The sword had made its way through the armor and penetrated the monster's thick skull as it buried itself deep into The Screech's head. Angered by this, the monster intensified its efforts as it struggled to move forward. With each step, its growling becoming louder and louder. Within an instant, The Screech belched out an earth-shattering howl and started breathing fire!

"I told you it was a dragon!" Thomas said as he turned to his friends. "Watch out! He's getting ready to spit fire on me!"

Roland watched as a stream of fire burst from The Screech's mouth. "Get down low! Maybe you can hide in the mud!"

Thomas dropped into the watery sludge as the flames grew. He felt the intense heat raging as The Screech unleashed its anger. Louder and louder, the screaming intensified until it became still and silent. Everyone stayed frozen for a moment, staring at each other, waiting for The Screech to make its next move, but it never did. When nothing else happened, the small army of friends threw their arms in the air and cheered!

"You defeated it!" Roland yelled. "Well done, Sir Thomas of Creekside!"

"Way to go!" Roxanne said. "It must've lit itself on fire with its breath!"

Through dirt encrusted eyes, Thomas raised his head and watched as the massive flames engulfed the monster. The Screech wasn't moving.

"Teddy would be so proud," he said.

"Don't worry! We'll help get you out," Roxy said. "Roland, grab some rope from your house."

But before his friends had the chance to reach him, Thomas heard something sloshing through the sludge in the distance. He crouched down as low as he could to hide from this new threat until a glint of golden sparkles pierced through the thick, billowing smoke.

Thomas slowly raised his head and smiled. "It's her! The Golden Pixie. She's out here with us!"

In the midst of the dark smoke, a thick cloud of white powder burst out from the Golden Pixie's hands as the mythical goddess bravely walked toward the beast.

"She's casting a spell on The Screech!" Roland yelled as they watched the Golden Pixie conjure up clouds of magical fairy dust that she blasted on the monster.

The flames died down and the Golden Pixie thrust her hand into The Screech's lifeless body.

Thomas' jaw dropped. "I think she's ripping the monster's heart out."

The Golden Pixie yanked her hand back and, turning toward Thomas, he saw her gold light shimmering brighter as she approached him. As soon as she got close enough, he discovered her mystical secret. The brilliant light was coming from the sun, reflecting off a gold badge dangling from around her neck.

"Thomas? Is that you?" she asked. Her angelic voice echoing across the water.

The Golden Pixie knows my name, he thought.

"Yes," he said, using his blanket to wipe the dirt from his eyes.

"Thomas. I'm Detective Spillen. We've been looking for you for a few days. Everyone's been so worried. I'm going to take you home, okay? Your mom misses you so much!"

Thomas' eyes glistened, and then he realized something. "Wait, I know you. You came to my school to talk to us about being safe."

Detective Spillen smiled, trying to hold back her own tears. "I did. And obviously you are a super, good listener. Look how brave you've been! You are a true knight! Here, let me get you out of there, sweetie," she said as she reached for Thomas. "You're in there pretty deep, so I'm going to need both hands to get you out of this mud. Can you do me a huge favor and hold this for me?"

Bringing her other hand forward, she reached out to Thomas, and in her hand was a soiled blue bear with a red bowtie that smelled of smoke.

Thomas' mouth dropped and his eyes grew wide. "Teddy! You saved him from The Screech!" He grabbed hold of the bear and hugged him tight against his chest. "I've missed you so much, Buddy!"

"The Screech?"

"Yeah! The evil dragon," Thomas said, pointing toward the smoke. "Is it dead?"

Detective Spillen turned to the smoldering remnants of Krantz's van with the large wooden stick jutting out from the front of the engine. "Sweetie, you'll never have to worry about The Screech ever again."

ABOUT THE AUTHOR

Garrett first knew he wanted to be a writer when he was five-years-old. By the time he entered the second grade, he had his first story published in the local paper. It wouldn't be until many years later before he returned to writing.

During his hiatus, Garrett not only attended college, he joined the Florida Highway Patrol, and was later offered a position with the FBI. After his career as a Special Agent, spending most of his time investigating Counterterrorism threats, Garrett retired and once again returned to writing. Nowadays, you can find him at his home in Upstate New York crafting stories, keeping bees, boiling maple syrup, and a litany of other hobbies that will hopefully keep him from getting into mischief.

OTHER WORKS BY G.L. GARRETT

Keeper of the Hourglass: The Life and Death of Peter Nichols
Keeper of the Hourglass: Apius's Revenge
Keeper of the Hourglass: The Crimson Manifest

Thank you for reading and please check out my website:

https://www.glgarrett.com

The one and only, Theodore E. Bear,
aka Teddy

CPSIA information can be obtained
at www.ICGtesting.com
Printed in the USA
LVHW102047120922
728184LV00014B/217/J